The Dark at the End of the Tunnel

Taylor Grant

Crystal Lake Publishing
www.CrystalLakePub.com

To Samantha and Zane,
my lights at the end of the tunnel.

COPYRIGHT ACKNOWLEDGEMENTS

"Masks," *A Feast of Frights from the Horror Zine*, ed. Jeani Rector, Horror Zine, 2012; "The Silent Ones," *Horror For Good: A Charitable Anthology*, ed. Robert Shane Wilson, Mark Scioneaux, R.J. Cavender, Cutting Block Press, 2012; "The Vood," *Box of Delights*, ed. John Kenny, Aeon Press, 2012; "Gods and Devils," *Blood Type: An Anthology of Vampire SF*, ed. Robert Shane Wilson, Nightscape Press, 2014; "Dead Pull," *Tales from the Lake Vol.1*, ed. Joe Mynhardt, Crystal Lake Publishing 2014: "Show and Tell," *Night Terrors III*, ed. Theresa Dillon, Marc Ciccarone, G. Winston Hyatt, Blood Bound Books, 2014; "The Infected," *Cemetery Dance Magazine #71*, Cemetery Dance Publishing, 2014; "Whispers in the Trees, Screams in the Dark," *Nightscapes Vol. 1*, ed. Robert Shane Wilson, Marc Scioneaux, Jennifer Wilson, Nightscape Press, 2012; "Intruders," *Horror Library Vol. V*, ed. R.J. Cavender, Boyd E. Harris, Cutting Block Press, 2013; "The Dark at the End of the Tunnel," (appeared as "Specters") *Fear the Reaper*, ed. Joe Mynhardt, Crystal Lake Publishing, 2013.

Library of Congress Cataloging-in-Publication Data has been applied for.

"Taylor Grant is a bold, unsettling new voice in suspense and horror."

—Scott Nicholson,
Bestselling Thriller Author,
The Red Church

"As classic, elegant and as deadly effective and efficient as a switchblade, the stories here echo the timeless storytelling of The Twilight Zone, E.C. Horror comics, and 1980s paperback kings, while carving up their own new brand. Grant's collection will leave you with plenty of scars to show off around the next late night campfire."

—John Palisano,
Bram Stoker Award Finalist,
Dust of the Dead, Nerves

"Taylor Grant's style is crystal clear and scalpel sharp. These beautifully crafted tales culled from the deepest recesses of Grant's devious imagination feature an array of horrors, including faces shaped by our dark side yearnings, shadows baring sharp teeth (though the origin of these shadows is even more shocking), how a secret hidden away in a footlocker spreads like an infection, and even vampires at the far edge of the universe. Grant's obvious glee in depicting these horrors and more makes this collection a joy for the reader who enjoys the work of classic horror writers such as Richard Matheson and Stephen King. Yet it's his talent as a storyteller dealing with modern themes that lends these tales depth and humanity of which we all can relate. Highly recommended!"

—John Claude Smith,
Riding the Centipede, Autumn in the Abyss.

"A rip-roaring, fast-paced collection that nosedives the reader into a world of mind-busting terror and seduction; part these pages at your own risk, as Grant picks away at your worst fears . . . the bogeyman finally as a name . . ."
—David Owain Hughes,
Walled in, White Walls and Straightjackets

"Taylor Grant is a master at balancing pure dread with raw untethered emotion and brilliant characters in a complicated concoction of the best kind of horror. The kind of horror that gut punches you in vivid slow motion and leaves you breathless in its wake. Mark my words: he will leave an unmatched legacy in the genre."
—Robert S. Wilson,
Bram Stoker Award-nominated editor,
author of the *Empire of Blood* series

"These stories strike hard as steel and silent as a shadow's whisper—a cornucopia of horror from a master of the genre!"
—Tim Waggoner,
author of *Eat the Night* and *The Way of All Flesh*

CONTENTS

Foreword by Gene O'Neill...i

Introduction by Taylor Grant iii

Masks 1

The Silent Ones 16

The Vood...30

Gods and Devils...53

Dead Pull 80

Show and Tell 100

The Infected 115

Whispers in the Trees, Screams in the Dark 143

Intruders 167

The Dark at the End of the Tunnel 181

FOREWORD BY GENE O'NEILL

DIFFERENT TYPES OF writing require different subsets of writerly skills. Sometimes there is an overlap. But very seldom does a writer possess a high level of multiple skills in all types of writing. Some of the different skill sets are:

Playwrights and Screenwriters—The form requires exceptional skill at creating believable dialogue that moves the plot along.

Novelists—The form requires master planning of the big picture, juggling multiple storylines, and producing interesting exposition to inevitable conclusion.

Poets—The form requires precision and concision producing concrete imagery and emotional effect.

Short story writers—The form requires economic use of language—never an extra word—to produce a measured ending that has perfect closure.

Only the very best writers possess all these varied skills. These writers produce our most memorable literature—they are master craftsmen.

Taylor Grant possesses a good measure of all these skills, as one might expect because he has written at a professional level in many different mediums. The proof, of course, is in the quality of the short stories in this collection. Every story here is written with the precise-concise language of a poet; the dialogue is crafted at a screenwriter's level; the care and plotting is equal to a novelist; and each story has an almost perfect closure—often an unexpected but inevitable ending.

Some of the stories have an underlying psychological theme bordering on madness—the lead character psychotic or at the very least sociopathic. Yet this isn't just a collection about *bad guys*, oh no. We, as readers, are able to root for most of the protagonists . . . Or if we can't in a few cases, the endings are carefully ironic—the bad guy gets exactly what he deserves. A difficult technical writing skill is to always create a satisfying ending from the reader viewpoint. Each story ending here has that type of satisfactory conclusion.

Taylor Grant accomplishes all of this because he is a gifted writer, his skill set cutting across all the major forms of writing. Other writers and colleagues, too, recognize his ability. My favorite story of this collection, the novelette, *The Infected*, although competing against much longer novellas, was a finalist for the prestigious Bram Stoker Award in the Long Fiction category.

I would suggest that Mr. Grant's fiction will garner many such writer awards; and I wouldn't be surprised to see one or more of his stories produced on TV or the big screen in the near future.

Taylor Grant. Write the name down, seat it with a magnet on your refrigerator, and then watch it popping up all over the literary landscape.

Gene O'Neill,
Bram Stoker Award Winning Author,
The Cal Wild Chronicles, The Hitchhiking Effect
At the Lazy K

Introduction

I’M GOING TO tell you a secret.

You’re not supposed to be reading this. And I’m not supposed to be writing this introduction.

A strange way to introduce myself, I know—but it’s true. Most of the stories in this collection were not written for publication; rather they were written as my escape. An escape from the countless compromises I had to make as a writer in other industries, from the mundanities of life— and often from myself.

Here’s another secret: I didn’t want the rejection.

I had experienced enough of that working in the entertainment industry, where I spent years writing in a host of mediums, including film, television, radio, newspapers, magazines, and comics. I even wrote a couple of one-act plays that were performed in Los Angeles.

But despite some success as a screenwriter, rejection always lurks in the shadows of Hollywood, ready to pounce—it is the nature of the beast. So when I decided to start writing short stories for pure enjoyment, the idea of subjecting them to rejection by publishers seemed like the surest way to suck the joy right out of it.

So it began. In those rare moments of quietude amidst the merry-go-round of life, I wrote in secret and for fun. It was my personal rebellion against having to “write to market" in Hollywood. There was great creative freedom in not having to pay the rent with these stories. I didn't have to please my agent or studio execs either—I could pen whatever the hell I wanted.

My muse had rekindled the fire that excited me about creative writing in the first place—a fire that had sparked to life as a boy watching shows like *The Twilight Zone, The Outer Limits, Star Trek, Night Gallery,* and those wonderful made-for-television movies like *Duel, The Night Stalker, Trilogy of Terror, Gargoyles,* and *Don't Be Afraid of the Dark.*

This is why *Masks*—the opening story in this collection—has special significance to me. It was the first time I had written something that felt like my true creative voice. Of course, it wasn't the first time I'd tried my hand at short fiction. As a child I churned out a fair amount of poorly disguised imitations of movies and TV shows that I loved. And in my early twenties I attempted a few science fiction and horror tales that contained some intriguing elements, but ultimately felt like bad mimicry of authors I admired. Namely, members of the author collective referred to as "The California Group," a loose affiliation of friends that consisted of Ray Bradbury, Richard Matheson, Rod Serling, William F. Nolan, Charles Beaumont, Robert Bloch and several other brilliant writers.

When I sat down to write new stories a decade after the last attempt . . . something had changed. This time I wasn't trying to create something to sell nor was I trying to prove anything. I just wrote what inspired me without worrying about the most impressive word choices or finding the right turn of phrase. And lo and behold, out came a piece of fiction that contained many of the elements I've always enjoyed as a reader: an intriguing premise, an entertaining storyline, unexpected twists, and most importantly—a theme with something to say.

That first story was called *Masks*.

It immediately went into a drawer.

Over the next few years I wrote several more stories whenever inspiration struck. And like *Masks*, these stories enjoyed a nice long stay in a drawer or digital file folder on my computer.

Eventually, though—my oath of secrecy began to crumble. And it was without any planning or strategy that I shared a story or two with my wife and a few unsuspecting friends.

It was terribly nerve-wracking at first, for each story was like a piece of me; a little bit of magic I created when no one was looking or asking for it. These tales were sacred; they were my art. Not in a hoity-toity way, but more like a young child creating sculptures with mud for the first time. I was enjoying my sandbox and I didn't want anyone telling me how I should play with my sand.

The initial response to my fiction was positive and supportive. But being rather insecure about the merit of these stories, I told myself that everyone was just being kind. After all, they were unanimously kind people. And so, back into the drawer they went and back to writing I went— slowly, without any ambition to have them published.

I retired from my professional screenwriting career in 2005, after having the good fortune to write both animated and live action television shows, quite a few music videos that aired on MTV, and five movie projects at various Hollywood studios, including Universal, Lions Gate and Imagine Entertainment. (As so often happens in Hollywood, I was paid for my work, but none of the films made it into production).

That was the year my son was born, and I was determined to focus on fatherhood. It remains one of the best decisions I've ever made. So for the next five years I focused on my family and paid the bills writing marketing and advertising (Web, print, TV and radio).

Yet a little bit of my soul died every year that I didn't write fiction.

So, in early 2010, with the encouragement of some dear friends who enjoyed my work, I polished up all of my stories and did my best to make them worthy of publication. I submitted them to magazines and anthologies that I thought looked like a good match.

To my utter surprise and delight, I received my first acceptance shortly after, in a wonderful little anthology out of Ireland called *Box of Delights*, featuring several award-winning authors, including Steve Rasnic Tem, Mike Resnick, and Kristine Kathryn Rusch.

That story was *The Vood*, and I literally wept at my computer when I opened the acceptance email. After so many years of trying to please everyone else as a writer, it was overwhelming to have a story accepted that I wrote to please myself.

To my complete shock, I sold all of my existing stories over the next 36 months and wrote four new ones (*Show and Tell*, *Intruders*, *Gods and Devils*, and *The Dark at the End of the Tunnel*) that were also accepted. My fiction appeared in two Bram Stoker Award nominated anthologies, and also in the legendary *Cemetery Dance Magazine*—something I could only have fantasized about a short time before.

To my continued amazement, the story that appeared in Cemetery Dance—*The Infected*—received a Bram Stoker Award nomination, a great honor that I will never forget.

I tell you this because perhaps you are sitting on some

ambitions of your own. If so, I encourage you to blow the dust off of some of those old dreams, polish them up, and expose them to the world. You never know what might happen.

And that brings us to now, whenever now may be for you. I can't thank you enough for your interest in my work and I sincerely hope that you enjoy them as much as I enjoyed writing them. I like to think of this collection as a magical brew. It is sprinkled with the essence of both shattered dreams and dreams made manifest; a touch of death's lingering grief and the marvel of birth; a pinch of despair, a dash of joy, a sprinkle of loneliness, and a heaping scoop of sweat, tears and yes—even blood.

These raw ingredients were harvested from a wide range of life experience and emotions over a 15-year period of my life. And it is with these materials that I wove the tapestry of this collection. Like magic, these ideas and stories sprang from my imagination during some of the most difficult times of my life—as well as the greatest.

I have changed since writing the first of these stories, and if I tried to write any of them now, they wouldn't be the same. They are the product of very specific times in my life, and for that reason they are near and dear to me.

Yes, they were an escape into the dark wonderland of my mind. And I believe that in some ways, they saved the artist within me.

I hope they serve as an escape for you, too—into a fun, scary, melancholy, thrilling, dark and imaginative place. Furthermore my hope is that as you turn the pages you might see some of the world in ways you haven't seen them before.

Sit back now as I turn down the house lights and start the projector within the theater of your mind.

Taylor Grant

I hope you enjoy the show.

Taylor Grant,
Los Angeles, CA
October 2015

Masks

JONATHAN DABBED AT the blood on his neck and licked his crimson-stained fingertips, savoring the sharp, coppery taste.

"What the hell's taking so long?" Margaret yelled from outside the bathroom door. "I'm going to be late for my spinning class."

Startled from his reverie, Jonathan noticed his reflection in the mirror and recoiled at the face staring back. He'd never smiled like that in his life; it was more of a grimace.

"Hurry up, goddamn it," Margaret said, pounding on the door.

Jonathan's fists tightened. He forced himself to take a deep breath before opening the door. "Sorry, honey," he said, "I nicked myself shaving."

Margaret brushed past him, shoved him out the door, and slammed it so hard his scrotum tightened.

With a familiar sigh, he continued his morning routine.

Later, while crouched over his computer at work, Jonathan couldn't shake the disturbing reflection he'd seen in the bathroom mirror—and that horrible gash of a smile.

It's just work-related stress, he thought. *God, please let it be that.*

He couldn't take another year like the last—and he sure as hell couldn't afford the therapy, although it seemed clear he needed another session with Dr. Hatchman. He warmly recalled his former therapist's signature western wear, bushy white beard, and perpetually rosy cheeks. He looked like Santa Claus moonlighting as a country-western star.

Jonathan chuckled at the mental image, gradually returning to the job at hand. He attempted to analyze a spreadsheet of projected revenue figures for the next fiscal year, but found it impossible to focus. He glanced down and noticed his fingers tapping at the keyboard as if they belonged to someone else. The spreadsheet minimized on his screen and was replaced by a Web browser. Moments later, a parade of violent, sexual obscenities marched across his screen.

He felt the twisted grimace of a smile invading his lips once again. He sat immobile at his desk, both repulsed and intrigued by the imagery on the computer. It was like driving past a particularly gruesome car wreck, not wanting to look—yet unable to tear his eyes away.

And then he noticed his hands. *Jesus Christ, my skin looks like . . .*

"Mr. Bailey?" a soft voice beckoned.

Startled, Jonathan quickly minimized the images on his computer screen.

A petite brunette with perfect teeth to match her perfect smile peeked inside his office. "Mr. Bailey, your three o'clock is here."

"Thank you . . . " Jonathan's voice wasn't his. It was deeper. Colder. He cleared his throat and tried again. "Thank you, Jenny. Tell them I'll be just a moment."

She gave him a curious look. "Are you okay?"

"Fine," he lied. "I'm fine."

She raised her shoulders in that little shrug he hated and closed the door with a click.

"Whore," he heard himself mutter, feeling surprised at the venom of his tone.

He turned his hands palms up, then down, studying every inch. They appeared normal again. *It's just work-related stress*, he told himself for the second time that day.

He'd chewed two of his fingernails down to bloody nubs by seven o'clock that evening. He swore if he had to create one more Power Point presentation he was going to rip the skin from his bones. In an uncharacteristically bold move, he ignored a handful of last-minute email threads and left early.

Jonathan drove home, thinking about the bizarre events of the day with an increasing sense of unease. He longed for a session with Dr. Hatchman. Unfortunately, he'd already used up the allotment of counseling sessions his pathetic HMO covered. If he wanted to reenter therapy, he'd have to pay out of pocket—and he simply couldn't afford that. He and Margaret were hemorrhaging money due to her obsession with home renovation, and he didn't have the balls to stop her.

He forced a deep breath; he was probably over-dramatizing. End of the year was notoriously crazy and he was simply overworked. Hell, a weekend by the pool with a few dry martinis, and he'd feel like a new man.

Actually, I feel better already, he thought.

Suddenly, two teenage boys in a gray Impala cut him off. Jonathan instinctively jerked the wheel to the right and nearly lost control of his Taurus but was able to straighten out. The pimple-faced driver laughed at him and pressed his middle finger to the window.

Jonathan's fingers coiled around the steering wheel like tiny, hungry pythons as he slammed onto the accelerator. He raced up alongside the Impala, honking his horn viciously. As the boy glanced over, Jonathan was surprised to see the boy react in fright and swerve away.

It only heightened Jonathan's bloodlust; he veered toward the Impala even more aggressively. The pizza-faced driver panicked—weaving into the far lane.

But there was no far lane.

Jonathan caught a glimpse of the boys' faces frozen in screams as their car sailed off the road to be engulfed by the blackness below. The canyon was so deep that Jonathan didn't hear the impact.

He glanced up at the rearview mirror as he drove away, searching for any witnesses. He was relieved to see that the only visible headlights were tiny pinpricks—at least a mile in the distance. Whoever they were, they were too far off to have seen anything, much less identify his car.

He exited the road at the next turnoff and took a dizzying maze of side streets to get home. As he drove through a desolate warehouse district, he caught a glimpse of his frightful reflection in the rear view mirror—and nearly lost control of his car. The Taurus spun wildly as he careened over a hill. He slammed on the brakes, flung open the door and tumbled out onto the oil-stained asphalt.

Oh, God . . . Oh, Jesus . . . Oh, God, he thought, scrambling to his feet. His features had been horrifying, as if they were stretched over some monstrous *thing* beneath his skin. Is that what the boy had seen—why he'd looked so terrified?

He walked aimlessly along some long-forgotten railroad

tracks as the realization of what he'd done—the enormity of it all—began to sink in. He might have *killed* two young kids.

Wait, he thought. Temporary insanity. Yes—that would be his plea if he got caught. It made perfect sense. He'd already been through a nervous breakdown the previous year. Dr. Hatchman was a character witness; perhaps he could confirm that Jonathan had a pattern of psychosis. Would it be a far stretch to say that he'd never fully recovered? He played out every scenario he could think of.

He wandered silent streets until he'd formed what he thought was a reasonably convincing narrative. When he finally returned to his car, it took him an additional twenty minutes to find the courage to climb inside.

He avoided looking into the rearview mirror as he drove home.

~

Jonathan watched the evening news and scoured the morning paper for several days. He discovered the brief news item while eating breakfast. It was a missing person's story, with requisite quotes from worried family members and a reward offered for any information. As it turned out, fourteen-year-old Andy Creeter and seventeen-year-old Rusty Creeter—pizza-face himself—were brothers. The police considered it a runaway case due to the boys' past histories and juvenile records.

A conspiratorial grin crossed Jonathan's lips. There were no bodies, suspicions of foul play, motives to uncover, or any living witnesses. If there were such a thing as a perfect crime, this came pretty damned close.

He studied the news story for so long that his corn flakes fused into a single membrane floating aimlessly in his bowl. For a moment, he worried that Margaret might have noticed his preoccupation with the story—but she was far too busy renovating the kitchen.

While she savagely attacked some drywall with a chisel and hammer, he made his move toward the sink and dumped his bowl of mush into the disposal. He was about to leave for work when he heard Margaret mumble "Have a good day," with a distinct lack of interest.

He started to offer his automated response, "You, too," but was cut off by her vicious hammering. It seemed as if the only thing that interested Margaret these days was tearing things apart.

Within a few days, he'd put the whole dreary Creeter affair behind him. A voice inside his head offered constant reassurance; told him that everything would be just fine.

The voice wasn't his.

At work, others began to notice changes in Jonathan.-

The Tuesday morning executive meeting began as a typical corporate affair, with Don Henry, the company CEO pontificating about quarterly milestones and meeting stockholders' expectations. Don's formidable business acumen was second only to his quick-tempered nature. He had a reputation for verbally assaulting anyone who questioned his authority.

Jonathan sat in a cold sweat, fighting an overwhelming urge to leap across the table and rip the son of a bitch's tongue from his mouth. Adding to his discomfort was a strange and extraordinarily painful throbbing sensation in his lower back.

Eventually, Don called him out. "Is there a problem, Bailey?"

Jonathan dug his fingernails into his wrist to keep from laughing at the silver-haired man. When Don asked him again, Jonathan burst into such a howl of laughter that spittle flew from his mouth.

The veins pulsed in Don's neck. "What the hell's so funny?"

"You," Jonathan heard himself say. "If you think anyone in this room gives a rat's ass about meeting stockholders' expectations, then you're an even bigger corporate stooge than I thought."

Silence choked the room. All eyes bounced between Jonathan and Don Henry. No one knew how to react. No one dared make a sound. After an unbearably long moment, Don collected his charts. "See me in my office in five minutes," he said and left the room.

Jonathan snapped up his papers and started after Don, feeling the entire room staring into his back. As he reached the door, he turned to Peter McIntyre, a particularly sycophantic Director of Marketing, and *snarled* at him.

Peter turned white.

Jonathan could still hear nervous laughter from the conference room as he reached Don Henry's palatial corner office. He didn't bother to knock.

Don stood before a large bay window, staring out at a spectacular panorama of the city. His voice was solemn. "Have a seat."

Jonathan plopped into one of the designer guest chairs and winced from an electric jolt to his tailbone. Don circled like a pin-striped predator sizing up its prey. "You've seen the African masks on the wall behind my desk?"

Jonathan grunted; everyone in the office knew of Don's collection of crude wooden masks and his oft-told tales of traveling through the Dark Continent. Each mask represented a different human expression: joy, sadness, lust, anger . . . the entire spectrum.

Don gave Jonathan a furtive glance as he stepped behind his massive oak desk. "Ancient tribesmen believed that by wearing one, you could draw power from the expression it represented." He removed an angry mask from the wall, appeared to silently address it, and then peered at Jonathan through the eye slits.

"You have a mask, Bailey. And it's cracking. I can see it happening . . . hell, everyone can see it. Things have never been quite right since your . . . 'episode' last year."

Jonathan thought: *Oh, but it's your mask that's cracking, Don. I can see the fearful little creature behind the puffed-up façade.*

He leaned forward, matching Don's steely gaze; he was still surprised by his own audacity. "What's your point?"

"My point," Don said with a nervous tic in his eye, "is that I don't want you anywhere near me or this office when you finally crack apart."

Jonathan rose to face Don. "You talk a lot about me and my mask, old boy, but what about yours?"

"Excuse me?"

"You're a frightened little man," Jonathan heard himself say, "hiding behind your self-important position like a child hides behind his mother's knees." He took several steps forward, moving around the desk toward Don.

Don took an involuntary step back.

Jonathan grinned, but there was no warmth there. "You know that beneath this pretense of boss and subordinate, we're no different than wild beasts back in the jungle."

Don's face was turning ashen. "What the hell are you talking about?"

Jonathan took another step forward, tightening his fists. "The truth scares you, doesn't it, Don?"

Suddenly, Don's knees buckled and he stumbled back into his custom-made leather chair, gasping for breath. Jonathan loomed over him, well aware of Don's history of heart trouble, including two heart attacks and triple bypass surgery. He leaned in and bared his teeth for effect. "Because once you lose your perceived advantage, you know I'll eat you alive."

"Get out!" Don wheezed, clutching at his left arm. "You're fired!" His face was covered with sweat, twitching wildly. He tried to reach for his phone, but Jonathan stood in his way.

"You were right, Don. My mask *has* cracked. Wanna see behind it?"

Don looked into Jonathan's eyes and gaped in horror.

When Jonathan stepped out of Don's office a few moments later, he smoothed the sweaty, tousled hair back from his brow and adjusted his tie. He sauntered toward Don's assistant's desk, where Meg, a stony-faced woman glanced up.

"You might want to check on your boss," Jonathan said casually. "He's not looking so hot." And then he strolled off toward his office.

He took his time packing his personal belongings into a box. There were several professional keepsakes, a withered office plant, and a framed photo of him and Margaret with obligatory smiles. He carried the box into the hallway just outside his office and dumped everything into a nearby recycling bin.

He continued toward the building's main entrance and noticed a crowd of coworkers. The double doors at the end of the corridor were open, and the light of an ambulance beyond it pulsed like an artery, bathing the lobby with the color of blood.

As Jonathan reached the crowded room, coworkers began to whisper like schoolchildren. Jonathan glanced outside as two paramedics carried a stretcher with Don Henry on it toward the ambulance. He locked eyes with Don, who was alive, but seemed unable to speak. Don's face was frozen into a mask of terror, the result of what appeared to be a massive stroke.

Meg stood near Jonathan, her eyes dark with worry. "What the hell happened in there?"

Jonathan didn't answer. He just watched Don being loaded into the ambulance and tried his best not to grin.

As he drove to his physician's office a few hours later, Jonathan tried to convince himself that he was still in complete control. But the truth was that he'd been unable to suppress his wild ravings in Don's office. It was as if he were watching from outside himself, helpless against his baser instincts.

A sharp jolt in his lower back made him speed even faster.

~~~

"Very unusual . . . " Dr. Stanton mumbled as he studied Jonathan's X-rays.

Jonathan shuffled across the antiseptic room, rubbing his back. His eyes followed Dr. Stanton's finger as he pointed at a bizarre growth toward the bottom of Jonathan's spinal column.

He was almost afraid to ask, "What is it? A tumor?"

Stanton leaned in for a closer look at the X-ray. "Too early to say. If it wasn't so ridiculous, I'd swear your coccyx is *growing*."

"What's the hell's a coccyx?"

"Your tailbone," Stanton said, clearly as puzzled as Jonathan.
~~~

An hour later, Jonathan limped out of the doctor's office. Stanton gave him a prescription for some heavy-duty painkillers and told him to make an appointment with a specialist.

~~~

Every facet of Jonathan's life was spiraling out of control: his career, his marriage, his mind—and now his own body. Desperate for pain relief, he raced to the nearest pharmacy to fill his prescription.

It was early evening when he reached the quiet streets and perfectly groomed lawns of his neighborhood. The medication had kicked in rather nicely, turning his sharp pains into dull aches.

As Jonathan drove through the streets of the planned community, past the familiar imported trees, man-made ponds, and uniformly designed homes, he felt strange, like an outsider in his own life. What had once felt comfortable and safe now seemed oppressive; a prison of cookie-cutter suburban conformity.

He felt a renewed pain in his coccyx area, and recalled something he'd learned as a boy in science class. The tailbone—according to some evolutionists—was a leftover from man's early origins. He imagined himself growing a tail and regressing into some form of primordial beast. Turning into . . . *Oh shut up, you idiot.*

He reached his home, a nondescript box in an endless row of tract housing. As he pulled into the driveway, he caught sight of Margaret walking past a tall casement window facing the street. She was going to bed and wore a short plaid nightshirt; her long, sinewy legs looked remarkably sexy. Jonathan imagined them wrapped around his waist as he thrust into her like a frenzied animal. Despite
~~~

the medication, he felt a rise in his pants. It was a pleasant surprise.

By the time he reached the master bedroom, Margaret was feigning sleep. It was a familiar routine: he'd climb into bed and lightly kiss her cheek, her neck, and gradually move down to her shoulder. On rare occasions, she would stir, which was the green light for sex. Otherwise, she'd lie as stiff as rigor mortis.

As Jonathan reached her shoulder, it was obvious that this was going to be another *Night of the Living Dead*. He was disappointed, but not surprised. They hadn't had sex in nearly a year. After undressing, he lay down next to her and stared at the white, spackled ceiling. His thoughts drifted to Don Henry's words.

Your mask is cracking . . .

Is it? Jonathan wondered. And if it was, what was underneath? He suspected it was something terrible.

He mused about the people in his life, Margaret foremost in his mind. They'd been married for over a decade, and yet he often wondered if he knew her at all. He tried to remember what had attracted them to each other in the first place, but the memory remained elusive.

He thought of his neighbors and former coworkers as they prepared for work each morning: dressed in their power ties and corporate-branded uniforms. They were, of course, expected to act accordingly; a perpetual 9-to-5 masquerade ball—costumes and masks required. He also wondered about the people he passed on the streets, in the stores, and throughout the goings-on of his daily life. What lurked beneath their cool exteriors?

He recalled a recent news story about a beloved cardinal in New York who'd sodomized two generations of young boys, and the respected female pediatrician in Maine who was caught torturing infants under her care.

What lies beneath their masks? Or mine?

Rusty Creeter had seen it, and so had Don Henry. And Christ, look what happened to them.

He could feel something dark, twisted, and irresistible growing inside him. It smashed its fists against an invisible wall in his mind. A wave of fear washed over Jonathan, unlike anything he'd ever known.

Something wanted out.

He gripped the sheets defensively, eyes wide, feeling his control slipping away-

Margaret stirred with a soft moan. Jonathan held his breath, praying she wouldn't touch him. He knew he couldn't hold back whatever raged inside. But she rubbed an inviting hand across his leg and whispered, "It's time. I've been waiting."

Jonathan couldn't imagine what had prompted this, but then realized that it wasn't him that had aroused her. It was *something else.* As if possessed, he reached over and tore off her shirt, fully exposing her. She groaned with pleasure as he grabbed and clawed at her soft flesh. She responded in kind, biting his shoulder hard enough to draw blood.

She pounded at his chest and let him fill her with his desperate need. They had sex like wild beasts, biting, scratching, and tearing at each other. It was as if a storm had filled the room, whisking away the years of quiet desperation and long-suffered deceptions. In a perverse way, they seemed to be relating for the first time.

Their frenzied session went on and on, until Jonathan's adrenaline waned. The moment he regained control of his urges, he forced himself off of Margaret and tumbled to the floor in a bruised and bloody heap.

Margaret remained naked and sprawled out on the bed as Jonathan struggled to his feet. She smiled at him in a way he'd never seen before. There was a secret anticipation in her eyes. She seemed to know something—*see something*—he dared not imagine. Her unblinking eyes followed him as he limped into the bathroom and fell back against the closed door.

Glancing at the bathroom mirror, he gasped out loud. What he saw in the reflection was far worse than the blood and contusions.

His eyes . . . *Its* eyes. Whatever it was studied his pale reflection in the mirror with a mixture of revulsion and hatred. It glared at him from behind his own eyes.

And suddenly he understood.

The weight of this realization made his knees weaken. He grasped the bathroom sink to steady himself.

There had never been an *It* trying to take control of his life.

He *was* It.

He stared at his mask in the bathroom mirror as the fingers of his right hand grew talon-like. It began to tear jagged holes into his face. The severed flesh of his right cheek fell into the sink with a crimson plop.

I've been waiting. Margaret's whisper still echoed in his mind.

Yes, he thought. She was waiting for me to realize what she already knew.

The last of Jonathan Bailey watched as his scalp was separated from his skull and his eyes were ripped from their sockets. The metamorphosis was torturous but blessedly quick; Jonathan's bodily remains littered the floor like the sodden scraps of a slaughterhouse. Wet, jagged shards of skin from his legs and arms hung from the sink like laundry washed in blood.

It took a deep, rasping breath then, breathing freely for the first time. A female voice called out from the bedroom, and It grunted with feverish expectancy. Glancing into the mirror, It was pleased with the reflection staring back. It flashed a savage smile, tearing away the final strips of Jonathan's flesh with Its prehensile tail.

Entering the darkened bedroom, It saw a nude silhouette standing motionless—watching It from the shadows. It heard a squish and looked down to see the fleshy remnants of Margaret Bailey lying under Its feet: a lacerated ear, a mangled breast, and chunks of indistinguishable meat spread across the crimson-soaked carpet.

The thing that was once Margaret slithered out of the darkness with welcoming arms and a blood-soaked smile.

THE SILENT ONES

THE PHENOMENON WAS like a cancerous growth: imperceptible at first, yet silently spreading with lethal intensity. The first sign of something amiss was a noticeable lack of mail being delivered over the course of several months. One day it simply occurred to me that my mailbox was empty more often than not. Even local ads and flyers had stopped. I checked with the post office several times but they always had my correct name and address on file. Although each time I spoke with them it seemed to take them a little longer to find it.

I never would've believed that I'd miss junk mail, but I discovered that there was something comforting about seeing your name on a mailing label. It let you know that someone—even an automated mailing service—acknowledged your existence.

The last piece of mail I received was the week of Christmas. I was excited, because I could always count on holiday cards from my mother and younger sister Karen. Mom's cards were always sappy and included an awkwardly written personal note, while Karen's were always of the homogenized, humorous variety; your typical mass-produced greeting card.

It was Friday, December twenty-fourth, when I looked into my mailbox for the last time that side of the New Year.

Inside, I discovered a single handwritten envelope. An honest to goodness letter! I actually flushed for a moment at the prospect of sitting down to read it. After all, in those days of emails, texts and instant messages, who wrote letters anymore?

But as I read the envelope I felt the blood drain from my face.

The letter was addressed to my neighbor. The postman had put it in my mailbox by mistake.

After that, things worsened. A few weeks later, I called my mother to wish her a Happy Birthday.

"Hello?" she answered, sounding distracted.

"It's me, mom," I said.

"Can I call you back?" she replied in a way that told me she'd most likely forget.

I started to say "I love you," but she hung up on me.

I never spoke to her again.

Then my phone stopped ringing. I still got a dial tone when I picked up the receiver and could call out just fine. But no one called me. Not even those automated reminders for overdue bills.

It was quite humiliating coming home night after night to an answering machine that blinked zero at me. Sometimes I'd press the play button just to hear the automated recording, informing me that there are *no* new messages.

But at least it was a voice.

I even began to regret signing up for the national "do not call list" registry, which banned telemarketers. At that point, even a canned sales pitch would have been welcome.

There had to be some sort of logical explanation. I was a pretty rational person. My approach to life was methodical, particularly at my job where I analyzed insurance claims.

Initially, I approached my situation the way I did most things: systematically. First I checked for any issues with the phone company. Next, I called every company that I did business with or that I owed money. Oddly, I was unable to find any problems within any line of communication.

Every billing representative that I spoke with assured me that they would resend my bills—but for some reason they never did.

Every facet of my life became infected. At work I "slipped people's minds" on a regular basis. Missed appointments became the status quo, and people ignored me wherever I went.

I got so pissed off that I decided to skip work without telling anyone.

It was the first time I'd ever done that. I even planned it so I'd miss my yearly evaluation from my boss, just to make sure my absence would be noticed.

It wasn't and he didn't. In fact, no one did.

Fifteen years I'd dedicated to that company. And not a single person noticed I was gone.

Any attempts I made to reconnect with the world were met with a wall of indifference. At first, I tried being overtly nice to everyone, starting with my obnoxious, two-packs-a-day, neighbor who sat on his porch most of the day blowing secondhand smoke through my living room window. When that didn't work, I tried being friendly to the forever imposed upon barista at my local coffee house. Her stoney-faced visage spoke of a childhood devoid of smiles. I also tried my snot-nosed cubicle mate at work and the Chinese food delivery guy with the terminal case of halitosis.

It made no difference.

When the niceties failed, I became overtly nasty. I shot people dirty looks, spat at others, even yelled at a few strangers for no other reason than to elicit a response.

No one blinked an eye.

Out of frustration I threw a full-blown temper tantrum right in the middle of our Thursday afternoon staff meeting, just to get a rise out of someone . . . anyone.

Having failed to interject a single word into the discussion, I screamed at the top of my lungs, "Excuse me!"

Kevin, the lead financial analyst sitting next to me, winced a bit at the sound of my voice, but kept right on talking. Finally, I heaved my hot latte, cup and all, as hard as I could against the far wall.

Suddenly, I had everybody's attention.

"Did you just throw that?" my boss, Barry said.

"Umm . . . yes," I said, suddenly wishing to God I hadn't.

"Why would you do that?" Kevin asked, but there was no judgment in his eyes. It seemed to be an honest question.

I started to stammer out a poor excuse for an answer. But within a matter of seconds, I was forgotten again. It was as if I could only maintain their interest for mere moments with the greatest of outrage and passion— emotions that I normally bottled up and rarely exhibited.

I panicked at that point and ran down the halls like a lunatic under a full moon. My wild energy provoked a smattering of human response, but not much more than if I were a monkey performing at the zoo, caged behind a sheet of impenetrable glass. It proved impossible to maintain such impassioned feelings. They were like unused muscles that had atrophied; the result of a lifetime of my own passivity and apathy. I was quickly disregarded; left alone to sob on the orange and puke brown carpet outside my cubicle.

A little while later, I gathered the wherewithal to drag myself home.

But sitting in my apartment was like solitary confinement. As I paced the floor, I thought I was going to lose my mind.

I had to find a way to engage with someone.

There was this gloomy 24-hour coffee shop down the street where local night owls perched every evening. I'd passed it countless times before, but had never felt compelled to go inside.

Until then.

I sat there for hours, soaking up the greasy walls of the dimly lit coffee shop, watching nothing but nameless faces with sunken, hopeless eyes. They seemed to be drawn to the place, like moths ticking at light bulbs. A grizzled waitress with a blank expression wafted across the floor like a specter, while the brooding clientele stared silently from the shadows.

Sometimes, while passing by late at night, I'd wondered what kind of people lurked inside this place at such an ungodly hour. Now—I was one of them. One of *them*: the silent ones; the nameless and forgotten; the in-between people that no one saw; the homeless that businessmen stepped over to get to their power lunches; the faceless figures that simply—filled up space and nothing more.

Somehow I'd become one of them.

I knew this because, for the first time in weeks—I'd been finally acknowledged. They seemed to recognize me. With a slight nod of the head or a weary meeting of the eyes, my status had been established. I was one of *them* now.

I watched them gather there all night, hovering quietly at their tables, comforted by the fact that they were not alone in their—our—misery. I had to get the hell out of there while I could. I may have been offered membership into the dead-end club, but that didn't mean I had to accept it.

〰

I didn't go back to work. No one noticed my presence, so I doubted they'd notice my absence. Money wasn't a problem, of course. I could steal any store blind and no one would raise an eyebrow. I wish I could say that provided me with some comfort.

I roamed the streets all week, searching for human connection. The city seemed . . . different: almost unrecognizable. Then again, perhaps it was my growing appreciation for things. Oddly, I'd never noticed the snow-dusted desert ranges, or the tall cacti that stood sentinel in the shadows of the great mountains. I was also surprised to see such a diversity of architecture pervade the city. I heard countless birds for the first time, chirping their esoteric songs from faraway places.

New scents and fragrant flowers seemed to permeate the air wherever I walked, and the endless blue of the September sky awed me.

However, what struck me the most were the people on the streets that I used to take for granted. They were filled with an energy that I found almost impossible to describe. Children glowed with it, like tiny suns. The adults and the elderly, I observed, shone with varying degrees of this radiant light.

Whatever this energy was, I envied it. When I gazed at my own reflection, I saw none. The other silent ones were also devoid of this radiance. We shuffled through the city unseen, except by our own kind.

I suspected that I might be dead—a wandering spirit perhaps. But neither of those conclusions made sense. I had yet to see a single indication of my death: a cleared out desk at my office; a boxed up and emptied apartment; a cheap funeral with a handful of detached mourners. But there was nothing.

The world remained unaware of my disappearance.

One day I walked through a local cemetery, searching for some peace of mind. My family plot had been there for years, passed down for three generations—a giant cavity in the earth, waiting patiently for its next meal. Everyone dead in my family was accounted for there.

I was relieved not to see a tombstone bearing my name. But the relief was short-lived, for it dawned on me that I hadn't consumed anything, neither food nor water, in several days.

Somehow, I had been subsisting on . . . nothing.

I was not dead. I was not a ghost.

I feared I had become something far worse.

***

It had been well over a week since I had gotten out of bed at home. By that stage I had memorized every crack, fissure and imperfection in the ceiling. I had yet to sleep, eat, or even relieve myself. But all of that seemed as meaningless as my life.

Now that the distractions of life had fallen away, the inevitable introspection appeared like an unwanted guest. The inescapable questions came up: What was my legacy? What had I contributed? Who the hell cared if I lived or died?

The weight of the answers had trapped me in this bed, sweating and stinking in a pool of regret. I found myself flipping through the pages of my past to discover a mental scrapbook filled with empty paper. I returned again and again to the same forgotten dream—eons ago—before the mundanities of life had slowly pushed it aside.

I once dreamt of being a man with something to say.

I saw a lovely face, peering at me through the veil of the past. Her name was Mrs. Wainwright—my exceptionally well-endowed grade school teacher. She often praised my flair for words. And that flattery led to my naïve, but wondrous fantasies about writing the great American novel (as well as fondling Mrs. Wainwright's breasts).

However, I was from a family of accountants, bankers, and financial analysts who not only scoffed at the idea of writing for a living, they made sure to humiliate me for even considering it.

I didn't have the fortitude to disagree.

Eventually my great dream faded into nothingness.

And now my very physicality, my very essence was joining that faded dream.

I shot myself in the face with a 12 gauge rifle.

I stole it from a local gun shop, came home, wedged it against the corner of my nightstand, stuffed the barrel into my mouth—and pulled the trigger. There was a vicious explosion as the world turned blindingly white—followed by impenetrable black. When I regained consciousness I was face down in a soup of blood, flesh and bone.

By all known laws of this universe, I should have been dead. I couldn't understand what was happening to me. It was as if this new existence wouldn't *allow* me to die.

With my remaining eye I could still see dried scraps of my brain coagulated on the wall across the room. The reflection staring back at me in the bathroom mirror made me vomit into the sink. My tongue dangled from my mouth like a dried-up, broken swing and pieces of my skull jutted from my face like shards of crimson glass.

If there was a hell, I prayed I'd find it soon. Even the devil himself would have been welcome company in such a lonely room.

~

I had become a human moth.

I swore I wouldn't return to the Godforsaken coffee shop, yet there I was again amongst those pathetic souls and that oppressive silence.

I was no longer allowed in the main eating and drinking area. When I stepped through the front door I was immediately directed towards a back room by a large and unfriendly fellow who practically shoved me inside.

This dark, smoke-filled room was smaller and even more congested than the main coffee shop. The silent ones back here were a whole other level of afflicted and forlorn.

My shocking visage didn't seem to bother anyone except me. As a matter of fact, this night's particularly vile looking crowd was riddled with what looked like failed suicide attempts. The blonde perched next to me at the tiny bar looked as though she may have been attractive once. But the precious reservoir of blood that pumped through her veins was long dried up. I could see crusted bones and shredded muscle through the tattered skin of her wrists: she had ripped them open with very little grace.

Worse off were two grim figures directly across from me: an obscenely bloated man who cradled his decapitated head under his arm like a mangled pet cat, and a figure to his right with skin so horribly burned I couldn't ascertain its gender. If you listened closely you could hear the seared flesh crackle and pop as it moved. Another gruesome character slithered across the floor like a human snake, his body reduced to a fleshy pulp—presumably after taking a nosedive off a very tall building. I nearly retched watching his shredded web of entrails drag after him on the dirt-encrusted floor.

But the worst by far was the festering abomination propped against the wall in the far corner. It was impossible to describe him/her/it. But the wretched thing was so dreadful that even the regulars wouldn't go near it.

I stepped past it later, as I moved toward the back door and heard what sounded like whimpers coming from what might have been a mouth once.

I wanted to scream at the sight of it, but I never got the chance. Just then a tall brunette woman stepped up to me and gave me the once over.

"Hello," she said.

For a brief moment I felt a rush of gratitude. I was so stunned that someone had spoken to me that I took an involuntary step back.

"Hel . . . hello," I replied. Or would have if it had been physically possible; my tongue was still hanging loosely from the cavity where my mouth used to be. And yet, somehow, I had communicated this simple greeting.

"You're new." the woman said matter-of-factly. She was probably in her mid-40s and had been attractive once. Her mouth didn't move when she spoke, nor did her awkwardly positioned head. It appeared as if she'd been in a serious car accident and broken her neck. I found it difficult to look her in the eyes, since they were practically vertical.

"I can hear you, but you're not talking . . . "

"That's the way it works here."

"Here?" What . . . what is this place?"

"No one knows," she said with no emotion. "A place for lost lives, perhaps."

She smiled at me then. The smile of a madwoman.

I took another step back, wanting to be anywhere but in this hellhole of a room. A man could go mad here. Clearly, some of the denizens already had.

When I left, I knew it would be for the last time. Loneliness may be hell, but it was better than facing those *things* night after night.

<center>~~~</center>

My life once again consisted of an empty apartment and my tedious reflections, countless days wishing for something—*anything*—to happen.

And finally, something did.

A young couple named James and Susan McIntyre moved into, or rather *invaded* my apartment. It had been vacant for a good while (I simply came home one day to find my personal belongings gone), so I suppose an intrusion like this was inevitable. I admit that, at first, I was thrilled. Their presence added some much needed color to what was beginning to feel like my own personal mausoleum. I followed them from room to room for days, listening to their intimate conversations like a man-sized fly on the wall. Sometimes I would lie next to them as they made love, trying to recall the fading memory of that experience myself.

During one particularly passionate session, I couldn't stop myself from reaching out to touch Susan. I was transfixed by her gorgeous auburn hair, which glistened with the sweat born of their lovemaking.

Her eyes locked with mine and she *saw* me.

She screamed, as I'd never heard anyone scream before. And it took her husband all night to calm her down and convince her that it was just her imagination.

Fortunately, she hasn't been able to see me since.

The weeks passed and I often huddled close to them as they talked into the wee hours, discussing the future and relishing their possibilities. Possibilities I once had, failed to notice and carelessly threw away.

One night, Susan discovered an old picture of me that had been wedged in a crevice on the top shelf of the bedroom closet. She didn't recognize me, of course, and tossed it into the garbage, where it sat for several days unnoticed.

But I noticed. I noticed how the image began to fade once it had been discarded. And by the second day, my image had vanished completely.

It was as if reality itself had forgotten me.

Any initial distractions the McIntyres' provided soon soured. Their joy had become my pain—their love my hate. They flaunted their lives before me with a constant torment of shameless affection. Now, when I saw them caress each other, I could only wish I *were* a ghost so I could haunt this place and force them from my home. But I remained invisible and powerless, unable to do anything but leave the last part of my previous life behind.

Perhaps it was for the best. Yes, maybe it was time to do something I should've done years ago: leave this city behind. Why not? It was high time I explored the world that lay beyond it.

How pathetic that this had only occurred to me now.

〜〜

I discovered that time had no meaning in this indeterminate state that is neither living nor dead. How long had it been now? Days? Weeks? Months?

It felt as if I'd walked several lifetimes, and yet, no matter how far I travelled—the past refused to be left behind.

However, there was something far more disturbing that I discovered during my trek. The world vanished around me with each step I took. The tastes and smells I once took for granted had now disappeared. The infinite sounds and countless textures of the earth were also gone—evaporated like yesterday's rain. As I walked, I would have given anything to hear my own footsteps again—anything to end the relentless drone of nothingness.

Though I clung to what was left of my sight, I noted that the once vibrant colors of the earth had fused into a dullish gray. My chance to experience all the wonders of the earth had simply . . . expired. There was no choice but to return to the city; there was no longer anything beyond it.

~~~

I am again in the darkened, back room of the coffee shop. The silent ones are all around me: the dispirited embodiment of countless promises unfulfilled, quiet desperations—and lost lives.

I glance from one hollow-eyed face to another and realize how desperately I will miss these silent figures—for the significance of their fellowship has become clear.

In some perverse way, they are here simply to connect—to bond with others somehow. They reach out to each other to keep from fading yet again—into an even deeper, more forsaken plane of existence than this one: an
~~~

unspeakably lonely place that awaits those of us who choose to isolate themselves.

This congregation of lost souls offered my last opportunity to avoid such a fate; a missed opportunity that I will regret for eternity.

I am fading fast, into a nether level that swallows me even now.

I am the festering abomination propped against the wall in the far corner—and even the silent ones don't notice me anymore . . .

THE VOOD

JESUS! IT'S RIGHT BEHIND–
No.

No, it was just a trick of the light, Grady thought. There weren't any shadows *anywhere.*

He had made damn sure of that.

He continued his sixth sweep of the apartment. He rechecked the army of lamps standing watch in his barren living room and inspected the reflective cloth fastened over each window. The duct tape was holding strong and every light bulb was in working order.

He winced at the onset of another tension headache. Sleep deprivation, of course. He couldn't remember what a good night's sleep felt like anymore. Perpetual artificial light combined with an incessant awareness of the Vood made sleep nearly impossible these days.

He weaved through the maze of floor lamps methodically, and then carefully inspected the single bedroom and closet-sized bathroom that completed his apartment. Track lighting along the ceiling and sconces along the walls created an onslaught of light from every direction. Their strategic positions were the result of hundreds of hours of trial and error. It had proven impossible to vanquish every single shadow, but the handful that survived were neutralized, surrounded and trapped forever within Grady's prison of light.

THE VOOD

After the final sweep was complete—the same routine for as long as he could remember—Grady collapsed onto the living room floor with a dull *thud*. Directly above him was an abstract pattern of cracked paint that spread across the width of the white spackled ceiling. It had more than a passing resemblance to a giant spider's web.

He stared at the weave-like pattern, imagining the last moments of a fly, knowing it is about to be eaten alive. He squeezed his red-rimmed eyes shut and tried to shake off the image. There was nothing left to do now but try and rest. He had ten long hours to kill before the sun would force the Vood back into the cracks and crevices of the world.

Grady knew virtually nothing about the homicidal thing. He'd nearly driven himself insane trying to uncover its secrets, scouring countless rare books on the occult, ancient mystical writings, and every corner of the Internet; he devoured any information he could scrounge up on demons, monsters and global folklore.

To date he'd come up with exactly *zero*. There wasn't a single reference in any known language. In fact, he could count what he knew about the Vood on two fingers: it liked to hide in dark spaces, and it had an insatiable appetite for human flesh. For this reason, Grady didn't venture outside after sundown. Any dark area could hide-

Stop it!

He curled up with a threadbare sheet and glanced around the room.

The one-bedroom apartment was nearly devoid of furniture, appliances, equipment or decorations—anything that might cast a shadow. The sole exceptions were his laptop computer, printer and portable 7" TV, which, due to their hard angles, managed to produce feeble shadows, despite the hoard of lamps that surrounded them. To counter this, Grady kept two high-powered Floor Sunlight Lamps angled toward him at all times.

Grady had also removed the doors from every cabinet and cupboard in his apartment, even the medicine cabinet in the bathroom. A specialty of the Vood—Grady had discovered—was hiding behind closed doors, even small ones.

For this reason, Grady had avoided dark spaces for most of his life; any garage, elevator or hallway could harbor unspeakable horrors. His long-departed refrigerator had nearly been the death of him during a particularly dreary night the previous December. He'd made the mistake of letting the automatic door light give him a false sense of security. A recurrent nightmare about being swallowed had awoken him that night, and he'd shuffled into the kitchen half-asleep. As he heated some chamomile tea to calm his nerves, he reached inside the refrigerator for a dash of milk.

Immediately, he noticed the burnt-out refrigerator light. But it was too late. A monstrous, gaping maw formed from the darkness and snapped onto his hand like a steel bear trap.

The pain was blinding; yet, far worse than the physical pain was the rape of his consciousness. The Vood had invaded his mind somehow, wailing its name so loudly that he couldn't hear his own screams.

For a brief but horrible moment, Grady *felt* its relentless, single-minded purpose: to consume. With the mad strength born of fear, he managed to wrench his hand free—though not all of it.

That was the last thing he remembered, until he awoke face down in a tacky pool of his own coppery-tasting blood, surprised to be alive.

THE VOOD

Grady stared at the jagged, pinkish scars of his mutilated right hand with a sense of fatalism deep in his belly . . . growing like a malignant tumor.

Grady's body jerked at a dark kaleidoscope of memories and he awoke with a start. He staggered into the kitchen and made some chamomile tea (he'd given up milk the night of the refrigerator incident) to calm his mind.

A vivid recollection from his dream caused tears to well up and spill from his eyes. In his mind, he could clearly see the warm smile of Bette Peyton, his beloved mother and a victim of the Vood.

As a child—before the creature had revealed its name—Grady had referred to it simply as *the Spot*, and he'd questioned whether or not it was just a figment of his imagination for some time.

His mother, much to his chagrin, found his prepubescent fears rather amusing.

"Don't worry, darlin'," she'd once said with a chuckle, simultaneously flipping a flapjack over on the stovetop. "We all catch odd things out of the corner of our eyes. Those dark spots that follow you are just tricks of the light. They're called optical illusions."

Though Grady was a child, he damn well knew the difference between reality and optical illusions. For hours each night he tossed and turned in his bed trying to catch the shadowy creature off-guard, desperate for a longer, closer look. But it was elusive, forever hovering on the edge of his peripheral vision. The faster he tried to catch a glimpse, the faster it moved away. It became an absurd game—like a dog chasing its tail.

But the game ended forever on a painfully cold October

day, three days before his tenth birthday. He'd been lost in thought, watching snowflakes dance playfully outside his bedroom window, when a curious noise caught his attention.

Cautiously, he followed the odd sounds into his mother's room.

The first thing he noticed was her favorite silver locket lying on the bed. To his knowledge, she never took it off. Even more unusual was that her left slipper—cornflower blue, except for shiny patches from excessive wear—had ended up on her pillow.

And then, something—perhaps an intuition—made him whirl around.

Something unseen seemed to leap back.

He reached for his mother's locket, fear clawing at him, when something just above the headboard caught his eye: an oddly shaped shadow looming on the wall.

It lunged at him, its mouth the size of a small cave.

Grady stumbled and fell flat on his back, which was the only thing that saved him. Impossibly, the creature distended its hideous maw even further. Inside that glistening cavity was something staring back at Grady, something that would haunt his thoughts and dreams for the rest of his life.

His mother's face.

Her body was gone; only the head remained. Her once long and beautiful auburn hair was wet with ichor and wrapped around her pale skin like blood-soaked snakes. A mewling sound escaped from Grady's throat, and he thought at that moment he might lose his mind.

The monster charged at him again, but his survival instinct kicked in; he dove for cover under the bed. Jagged teeth—the size of butcher's knives—snapped down inches from his face and he shrunk back from a blast of putrid breath, an unholy mix of fresh blood and decomposing flesh.

He gaped in horror under the bed, his tear-streaked cheek pressed to the hard wood as the creature began to alter its shape. A swirling pool of darkness formed on the floor nearby, and Grady realized that if he didn't move fast it would wash over him like a flash flood of black, gnashing death.

He scrambled out from under the bed, but was instantly jerked back under when the thing latched onto his left foot. He yelped as his tennis shoe was yanked off and he was suddenly free again. The relentless thing was right behind him as he tore out of the room, but it reeled back when he reached the well-lit hallway, as if it had received an electric shock.

Grady ran from his house with the kind of blind terror that only children can know. He didn't dare look back until he reached the sanctuary of a neighbor's house nearly a mile away.

A lanky detective, who sported an iron gray cowlick of hair over his forehead, spoke to Grady on several occasions during the investigation into his mother's disappearance. Grady told him everything he knew about the nightmarish creature that dwelled somewhere in the house. He explained how it could disguise itself as a shadow on the wall and had nearly swallowed him whole. Clearly, this is what had happened to his mother.

However, his fantastic story only seemed to aggravate the no-nonsense detective. Grady endured hours of analysis with child psychologists who assessed that he was in denial about being abandoned by his mother. They hypothesized that he fabricated the mythical creature as a subconscious defense mechanism.

Grady knew it was psychobabble, he just hadn't known the word for it yet. Eventually, he gave up trying to convince everyone of the truth.

The case went unsolved.

That was the beginning of Grady's lifelong struggle with the Vood; shortly after his first placement in a foster home—for he had no other family—he discovered that the relentless thing could follow him anywhere.

He ran away multiple times, bouncing from foster home to foster home, disappearing whenever the Vood appeared, terrified that anyone else close to him might be eaten, too. Eventually, he became a fulltime runaway; his days spent begging for money or pouring through books on myths and legends at the public library. At night he slept in train stations, subways, and brightly lit gas station bathrooms—anywhere that offered shelter with an abundance of light.

Unlike most of the kids he met on the street, Grady managed to stay clean. When he wasn't washing car windows for money, he spent his days at the public library and his nights hiding where he could. As years passed, he taught himself how to use the library's computers and discovered that he had a knack for programming. His talents enabled him to crawl his way up from the streets, and what was first a teenage hobby became a lucrative freelance business as an adult.

Working from home had been a strategic decision, as he knew he could never handle a job in a regular work environment. There were too many variables he couldn't control, too many places for the Vood to hide. And working in his shadowless apartment allowed him to avoid the natural but dangerous inquisitiveness of coworkers.

Grady discovered early in his life that maintaining any kind of relationship with friends or lovers was impossible. Certainly no one could understand, much less empathize with his predicament. And, of course, if he were to try and prove that the Vood existed to anyone, they would face terrible, unnecessary risk. He couldn't bear the guilt of anyone getting killed for something as selfish as his need for companionship.

Over the years, he'd found ways to cope with the interminable loneliness; TV personalities became his best friends and characters in pornographic films were his lovers. His only true companion was the Vood, and like a scorned lover, he knew it would never allow him to have a relationship with another.

As the years passed, the murderous thing became more and more aggressive. No longer content to taunt him from the corners of his peripheral vision, it stalked him openly from the shadows—ready to seize any opportunity when he might grow careless. Grady became a fugitive from his own life, moving from one place to the next, always trying to stay one step ahead of the darkness.

Always running.

But now Grady was fed up with running, tired of feeling like the nine year-old boy hiding underneath his mother's bed. He'd promised himself that he would not move again. Not from this apartment. Not ever. It was here that he would make his final stand.

～

The crashing footfalls of Grady's dream abated and he awoke, skin glistening with sweat. Fear, vague and undefined, crowded the edges of his consciousness, and the remnants of being chased still flashed in his mind.

A shadow crossed his field of vision and he heard movement from close behind. He spun to face a hulking figure looming over him.

Grady leapt back in a panic and knocked over his favorite lamp, a tall beauty with a carousel of bulbs. It crashed into four other lamps with a concussive domino effect. Grady scrambled to his feet with a mixture of anger, fear and outrage.

A fat, pallid face stared back at him. It was A.J. Feckler, the apartment manager. He wore a tiny pair of horn-rimmed glasses too small for his elephantine face. The man's skin was an unhealthy yellow and his fat lips curled over even yellower teeth when he spoke.

"Your rent's three weeks overdue," he said with a slight Southern accent. "I let myself in." His voice was deep and abrupt, like that of a former military man accustomed to command.

Grady felt sickened and violated, as if the Vood had taken the form of this jaundiced, obese man and invaded his home. He readjusted his sweat pants, which was all he wore, and began to set the fallen lamps upright. Two of them, he noticed, had broken bulbs, and the diminished light increased his nervous tension. "You have no right to enter my apartment without notice-"

Feckler cleared his throat of what sounded like a bowlful of phlegm. "I left notice. Three times. They're still taped to your front door."

"Still, you have no right-"

"I have *every* right. Check your leasin' agreement."

Feckler had him and he knew it. The roly-poly son of a bitch had him. "I'm working with my credit card company and—"

"Look, fuckwad." Feckler took a step forward, and all four of his chins jiggled when he spoke. "I don't give a dead moose's last shit about your shitty credit. I got fifty tenants with fifty tales 'o woe. Either you get me the money now . . . or your next notice is an eviction."

"Wait. Just . . . wait." Grady quickly calculated the cash he had on hand. It would cover his rent and enough food and supplies for a week—tops. It was the last of his savings; his conflict with the Vood had so consumed his life that his business was now in ruins, as were his finances.

"What's it gonna be?" Feckler said. His sneer became a look of apprehension as he glanced around, as if trying to comprehend the strange arrangement of lights that congested the living room.

"I have some cash. Wait here." Grady tried to maneuver around the grossly oversized man, but his arm brushed against Feckler's soft belly. It gave like a giant balloon filled with lumpy pudding. Grady swallowed in disgust and hurried towards his bedroom.

He'd nearly reached the short hallway when Feckler called out, "What's with the lamps? Goddamn fire hazard, you ask me."

Grady glanced back, "I'm a . . . lamp collector." He knew the idea was ridiculous even as he said it.

Feckler chuckled in his bulging throat and said, "How 'bout that. I'm a collector, too. Bullshit and excuses, mostly."

Grady glanced down and saw a pool of darkness spreading around Feckler's feet.

A shadow that wasn't a shadow at all.

Feckler noticed Grady's expression of horror and followed his eye line down. He immediately stumbled back as black, oozing matter surged up from the darkness.

My God, he *sees* it, Grady thought. And then he screamed, "Run!"

But the monstrous thing struck at Feckler with the speed of a cobra, engulfing his massive torso within its writhing darkness. Grady froze in horror, unable to move. His knees grew weak at the sound of the man's bones snapping—as if Feckler's body were caught in a giant wood chipper. His muffled shrieks could be heard beneath the blackish ooze as the Vood thrashed and gorged itself on his quivering mounds of flesh.

The loathsome thing grew larger as it feasted . . . and then it grew some more. Soon it filled the room like the smoke of an out-of-control fire. The echo of Feckler's bones being crushed reverberated through Grady's brain and gave him the determination to move. He grabbed his favorite lamp and thrust it forward, wielding it like a weapon.

He swung it at the murderous beast, the light slicing through it as easily as a sword through silk paper. The Vood immediately drew back, as if hurt. Grady took one guarded step toward it, empowered by his newfound weapon.

The dark thing retreated even more.

Mad laughter erupted from Grady's throat. He had it on the run for a change! He struck at it with the beam of light again and again, and it went berserk, like a gnashing tornado of black energy—terrifying in its intensity. But then slowly . . . reluctantly, it withdrew and shrank back, reminding Grady of what smoke looks like on film when it's shown in reverse.

Within moments the Vood was gone . . . along with any trace of A.J. Feckler.

〜

Grady spent the next three days vacillating between self-condemnation over Feckler's death and fear of answering for it. Torturous images of the fat man's demise replayed in his mind as he paced his apartment, often for hours at a time. Feckler had been an obnoxious, foul-smelling, Grade A asshole—but he hadn't deserved to die, especially as he did.

Hell, no one deserved a fate like that.

Sleep had been nearly impossible for Grady. At any moment, he expected a knock on the door from someone looking for Feckler—most likely the police.

Well, you see officers, he imagined himself saying. *There is this man-eating shadow that I keep at bay with my lamps. Here, let me turn down the lights and introduce you . . .*

But the knock never came.

By the end of the fourth day, he started to breathe a little easier. And by the fifth day, the sleep came a little easier, too. After all, if no one had seen or heard Feckler enter his apartment, no one should suspect him of any wrongdoing either. Grady didn't know any of his neighbors personally, but like most tenement dwellers, they seemed to prefer anonymity. Even if they had heard the scuffle in his apartment—hardly news in such a run-down dump—they would probably be reluctant to involve the police.

He'd already removed the rent due notices on his front door to avoid suspicion. And he'd increased his credit card limit by transferring a large amount to his last available card. His rent was covered—if only for the short-term.

That night he sent out some email queries to former clients, hoping they would forgive his months of lame excuses and general flakiness. *Sorry I've been out of touch*, he thought. *Been a little busy on this end, trying to avoid being eaten. I'm sure you can understand.*

When he could keep his eyes open no longer, he wrapped himself in a sheet and curled on the floor. As usual, sleep came hard. And when it finally did, the echoes of Feckler's muffled shrieks followed him into his dreams.

Grady took an inventory of his food and supplies with a sense of dread. He could no longer deny that he was in desperate need of both. With the Feckler incident weeks behind him, he realized he had no choice but to leave the safety of his apartment and head into the city. It was akin to walking through a giant minefield—even within the relative refuge of sunlight. The urban jungle cast shadows everywhere.

For the better part of a year, he'd figured out how to avoid the shadows of the outside world altogether. He'd had his groceries and supplies delivered from a local, family-run store and had made a deal with the perpetually red-cheeked delivery boy to collect and drop his mail each week for an extra five bucks.

His strategy had worked perfectly until one week prior when the store finally closed its doors, forced out of business by a larger, corporate-run supermarket. A supermarket that—according to the thinly disguised prick of a manager that Grady spoke to on multiple occasions—didn't do home deliveries, thank you very much.

Now, as Grady's eyes scanned his tiny kitchen, it was clear that he could no longer disregard the empty cupboards, nor his empty stomach. He quickly got dressed, taking note of the three remaining buttons on his weathered chambray work shirt. The lowest button hung by a single thread.

Symbolic of my life, he thought.

As he surveyed his apartment and considered the paucity of resources, he realized that being eaten by the Vood was the least of his problems. At this rate, he was more likely to starve to death.

Fighting monsters is exciting work, he mused with a macabre sense of humor, *but the pay is shit.*

He faced his front door on legs that trembled ever so slightly, knowing that if he didn't go at this very moment he might not have the strength—or the courage—to go later. He reached for the lock on his door and clenched his jaw so hard it clicked.

Moments later, he stood motionless in the darkened hallway.

Grady sometimes imagined that the path from his door, through the long hallway, and outside to the sidewalk beyond, had been purposely designed as a gauntlet of death. There were goddamn shadows *everywhere*. Of particular note was a menacing slash of darkness near the staircase that led to the second floor.

It looked like a malevolent smile.

Bite me, he thought petulantly and ran.

He sprinted through the hallway that never ended, leapt over the grinning shadow, and pushed even harder toward the porch, never looking back. He didn't dare stop until he'd reached the other side of the street.

"I . . . made it," he wheezed, offering his extended middle finger to the open door of his apartment building. "I made it . . . you son of a bitch!"

He whirled around, looking for anything suspicious, but the street was almost preternaturally quiet. There was only he, an old woman who looked like her face had been pinched by a giant hand, her Chihuahua taking a pea-sized dump, and a squirrel as big as the dog watching from the safety of a tree.

He didn't sense the Vood anywhere.

You can do this, said the voice in his head.

He forced his thousand-pound feet to move and began the five-block trek towards Mondo Market. His eyes darted back and forth as he walked along the cracked and pitted sidewalk, assessing each shadow that crossed his path. Every parked car, telephone pole and length of shrubbery offered a different-shaped threat.

He realized he might be a tad overcautious. The Vood could have been somewhere else entirely: another city or even another part of the world for all he knew. He often thought of this when it disappeared for what seemed like weeks at a time, as it had since the horrific Feckler episode. Perhaps it consumed other luckless souls in different time zones—when the night was young and the Vood was at its strongest.

Grady's focus shifted to his ill-fitting, second-hand tennis shoes that jutted out a bit too far in front of his much-too-short jeans. They slapped against the pavement in a rapid, steady cadence. The sun felt warm on his skin but he was unable to enjoy it, thinking only of the refuge of his apartment. His body was tensed to bolt and run as he carefully stepped around each shadow, although this slowed his pace considerably. To passersby, he imagined he appeared half-drunk or crazy, but he'd stopped worrying about other people's judgments long ago.

By the time he spotted the bright neon sign of Mondo Market, he was gasping for breath; too many years of inactivity, lack of sleep, and poor diet had taken their toll. Inside the store, the glow of florescent tubes cast a greenish-blue hue that gave everyone a washed-out, sickly appearance. Darkness was all but obliterated under the bright lights, but that was cold comfort; there was still the long walk back home, trying to juggle bags of groceries while avoiding shadows.

He gathered cans of soup (Mondo-branded tomato was a favorite, both cheap and good) and other non-refrigerated items. He could sense the eyes of other customers burning into him, but that was hardly a surprise; good grooming and personal hygiene had taken a back seat to survival over the past few months. Way, way back.

These were *normal* people, he thought enviously, thinking about *normal* things like their rising cholesterol, the rising cost of milk, and for the teenage boy he saw flipping through *Maxim* magazine—the rise in his pants.

He watched people tap at their wireless devices, yell at their kids, and dig for products with the best expiration dates. He noted how blissfully unaware they seemed; unaware of the fragility of their lives, and that despite ignorance, denial or both, death would eventually claim them all.

A portly man with a ten-dollar crew cut and his even fatter wife wheeled an overloaded shopping cart around him and hurriedly moved on, clearly uncomfortable under his scrutiny. He wondered what the rotund couple would do if they could see what death had in store for them. Would they overturn their cart of prepackaged poisons in horror and start eating sensibly? Or would they choose to hide from the world like him?

He recalled something from a book he'd read recently entitled *Mysterious Supernatural Phenomena*. The authors had claimed it was fairly common for the terminally ill, the extremely aged, and occasionally people found dying at the scene of an accident, to see what were called "messengers of death." The authors made the absurd postulation that they were angels or the spirits of loved ones, and that they helped the dying cross over.

Grady had hurled the book across the room in disgust. The schmaltzy, unsubstantiated conclusions were practically criminal, trying to delude readers into believing that these messengers of death were benevolent, simply because books about angels sold better than the cold, hard truth ever would.

However, of all the speculations in the book, there had been one that he agreed with: *that those who could perceive death were those closest to it.* It not only explained why Feckler had been able to see the Vood just before he died, but also why Grady had finally seen it on that fateful day in his mother's bedroom.

Somehow, he had escaped his fate that day. But apparently death didn't suffer unfinished business. It was relentless. It was unforgiving. And it had sharp, gnashing teeth.

Grady pushed his wobbling cart through an aisle that was stacked floor to ceiling with enough sugary treats to turn the entire country into diabetics. He didn't want to think anymore. He didn't want to theorize anymore. More than anything, he just wanted the comfort of some goddamn cream-filled cupcakes.

Grady stopped at the store's Customer Service booth before heading home and tried, for the second time, to convince the store manager—who wore a frozen mask of disinterest—to make an exception and deliver groceries to his apartment.

It was the same old story.

"I'm sorry, sir . . . but we don't offer those services here," the pasty man said as if there were a preprogrammed recording spewing from his mouth.

Disappointed and weary, Grady exited through a whoosh of the store's automatic doors. When he reached the street, he was hit with an unexpected blast of cold air. Up in the sky, a massive cloak of darkness had formed—skimming above the tops of buildings.

A whimper of panic escaped his throat.

No, he thought. *Please . . . not a storm today.*

His plea went unheard; a swarm of wrathful looking clouds suddenly devoured the sun.

Within moments, tenebrous fingers moved toward him, reaching from every direction, frantic and craving flesh. Grady lost control of his bladder and spilled his groceries. He literally ran for his life; the Vood's presence was everywhere, its hunger as palpable as the coldness in the air.

He didn't remember much after that, just bits and pieces of fragmented imagery—like a fever dream: a honking car . . . a hissing cat . . . horrified looks from bystanders as he tore past. Long tendrils of blackness clutched at his heels every step of the way.

He ran wildly . . . blindly, as he had those many years ago, when he'd first spotted the murderous thing in his mother's room. Not much had changed since then. His life was still a perpetual game of cat and mouse.

He was still forever on the run.

Grady awoke the next morning kissing the tile of his bathroom floor, where he'd passed out after regurgitating what felt like his entire large intestine. Weakened from hunger and nursing several pulled muscles in his legs, he found it a struggle just to climb to his feet. He groaned at a sharp spasm that clutched his left leg, and then groaned even louder at the memory of spilled groceries.

He limped into the living room and stopped so suddenly that anyone observing might have thought he had stepped into an invisible wall. What he saw there caused gooseflesh to ripple across his arms like a pool disturbed by a night's chill wind. Gone were the thin shafts of sunlight that normally peeked through the edges of his window coverings.

He glanced at his watch. It read: 11:00AM.

It couldn't be . . .

He hobbled to the nearest window with a grunt of agony and inspected the reflective cloth taped over it.

He looked at his watch again. The second hand still worked fine and the date was correct. Uneasily, he peeled a corner of duct tape from a window, peering out . . . eyes growing wide.

No! No no no . . .

He ripped away the cloth from every window, desperate to find a single ray of sunlight. He knocked over two floor lamps and his portable TV in the process, but didn't take notice.

Beyond his apartment there was only blackness, an endless, impenetrable thing that pressed against the windows with silent, deliberate breaths.

He dropped to his knees with a painful crack and began to sob uncontrollably. Not for himself—but for the rest of the world.

～

When the power to Grady's apartment died, he hadn't panicked; he'd been prepared for such an eventuality. He quickly mobilized three battery-powered lanterns, which managed to take the bite out of the darkness for a while. But after five of the longest days and nights of his life, the batteries were stone dead, and his backup candles weren't far behind. The remnants of six of them—melted, misshapen blobs now—formed a partial circle around him in the living room. The remaining five candles balanced their fragile flames over glistening pools of wax. Grady guessed he had less than an hour before those last, terrible flickers of light winked out.

The vantage point from the living-room windows revealed that an endless nightfall had befallen the earth; the Vood, it seemed, had become omnipresent. At first, Grady had imagined that it would come for him like a blood-crazed tsunami and carry him away.

Now, he wished that it would have. Anything would have been better than this.

The Vood had crept into his home insidiously and spread—like a field of malignant weeds. Savage attacks had come daily, sometimes more than once. A nibble here, and a nibble there; each one left him less of a man, and more of a mutilated thing.

Now, as he lay butchered and immobilized on the floor, he sensed it again; a formless malevolence that, if he looked closely enough, revealed hints of teeth and the barest outline of a grin.

It seemed to be playing with him, he thought, like a predator toying with its prey.

He caught a glimpse of his legs just then and the repulsiveness of it made him look away; they resembled two slabs of raw, gristly meat delivered fresh from the slaughterhouse. He closed his inflamed eyes and tried to ignore the sickening smell of blood that permeated the room.

For perhaps the thousandth time he pictured the end of everything, a surreal horror film stuck on a continual loop, projected onto the flickering screen of his mind. The opening scene was always the same: Grady trudged home from Mondo Market with a stuffed bag of groceries underneath each arm. He stopped suddenly as invisible claws of cold air raked across his skin. Then, gazing upward, he noticed an angry legion of storm clouds as they moved into position.

But as Grady studied the scene again and again, it had become clear that what he'd seen weren't storm clouds after all.

In that terrible moment, the Vood had spread across the sky like a cosmic bottle of ink spilled over the world. It consumed the great fire of the sun, and then, like some kind of celestial leech, sucked the blue right out the sky.

As far as the eye could see, the city was buried in shadow. And at that moment, Grady knew it was the beginning of the end.

So, he ran.

He ran and he ran.

And that was where his memory ended and his imagination began, a Grand Guignol of epic proportions as the Vood had its final, greatest feast—swimming through all of humanity in oceans of its own blood.

As he listened even now, there was nothing to be heard except the beat of his own heart. The world had been silenced forever. And somehow, the oppressive quiet was worse than a billion screams.

It had been inevitable, he supposed, that it would come down to this: just he and the Vood. And the loneliness of that thought was more painful than the tears and ruptures of his mangled flesh.

He forced his weary eyes open once again and gazed deeply, into the heart of the dark beast that filled the room. Immediately, he was struck by a disturbing sensation, an odd sense of . . . familiarity. There was a monstrous loneliness to the Vood that he knew all too well; a bottomless hollow that cried out to be filled.

Weakly, he reached out for it; his bloodstained index finger stretched just past the periphery of light. He watched, as that finger was torn away and swallowed.

The wail of the Vood's name echoed in his mind.

He saw the specter of his mother then, offering a lovely smile. It was a smile he craved more than anything as a boy, a smile that disappeared forever on the day she abandoned him to face the world alone.

Despite an agony so great it brought tears to his eyes, he pulled what remained of his body towards the glow of the last candles. It was as if he were watching from outside himself, his body propelled by a force not his own. Inch by inch, he dragged himself across the floor, painting it with what looked like the crimson abstractions of a crazed artist.

It was during these last moments of cognizance that Grady heard the Vood wailing in his mind clearly for the first time.

And finally, he understood.

Food is what his mind had been wailing all these years, not *Vood*.

FOOD . . . FOOD . . . FOOD . . .

Slowly. Deliberately. He blew out each candle.

Waiting for him was the darkness.

What the police found inside Grady's apartment caused the first uniform on the scene to race for the bathroom with his hand clutched over his mouth.

Now, as Detective Alfonso Guiterrez stood amidst the blood-drenched horror of the apartment, he was feeling a little sick himself. Loose, crimson-stained floorboards had already yielded several piles of human bones in various stages of decomposition, and the crime scene techs were just getting started. A majority of the bones, they noted, were marred with what looked like chew-mark patterns—like those on an eaten cob of corn.

In the bedroom closet they discovered a collection of heavy-duty trash bags bulging with putrefied human entrails. And so far, in the kitchen, he had seen three boiled human heads, and a miscellany of old bone fragments in a mixing bowl.

But that wasn't the worst of it.

The worst of it was sprawled just a few feet from Gutierrez; a poor excuse for a corpse that looked like it had been chewed up, partially digested and then spit back out.

He glanced down at the medical examiner hovering over Grady's remains.

"What do you think, Russell?" Gutierrez said.

Russell glanced up with eyes as lifeless as the body he examined. "Unofficially . . . asphyxiation. But I won't know anything for sure until we get him on the table."

"Asphyxiation from what?"

"Have a look," Russell said, prying open Grady's mouth with his gloved fingers.

" . . . the hell is that?" Gutierrez asked, already sure that he didn't want to know.

"Three severed fingers from his right hand," Russell said. "As far as I can tell . . . this guy tried to eat himself."

Gods and Devils

WHY CAN'T I *open my eyes?* Vega thought. *I'm not dreaming.*

Am I?

A single stab of pain shot through his arm to the marrow, followed by a rush of warmth. Then the rest of his body began to tingle. This was no dream. He'd been injected with something. He knew the feeling from back in Academy training; induced consciousness, only to be used in emergencies.

Next he felt an electrical impulse probing his brain, forcing his eyelids to flutter open.

His vision was blurry, but he recognized the porcelain, impossibly perfect features of Sona staring down at him. He took note that her right ear was missing, as well as some artificial flesh from her forehead.

A stronger electrical pulse now, coursing through his body, forcing his muscles to seize up for an agonizing moment. *This better be a goddamn emergency*, he thought.

He sat up with a groan and wiped temperature-regulating gel from his face. His eyes widened when he noticed the lower half of Sona was missing; it looked as if she'd been torn in two.

"Sona, what . . . ?"

Upon closer inspection, he could see that a large section

of her throat had been torn open—rendering her unable to speak.

Vega stared at her, wondering what might have caused such damage. Sona was a female droid, but she was built like a tank, complete with a dura-alloy chassis. She worked with quiet efficiency to disconnect him from the stasis field. As he rose to his feet, Vega grabbed the edges of the sleep pod for balance; his legs felt like they were made of pudding. Yet even hunched over, his six-foot five frame towered over the half-android.

He surveyed the stasis chamber. Everything appeared normal. Five hundred gleaming sleep pods, stacked ten rows tall, surrounded him. They were shaped like large silver eggs, containing humanity's last hope. Inside these pods were thirty-six crewmembers and four hundred and sixty-three passengers.

A nerve-grating sound caught his attention and he turned to see an awful sight. Sona was crawling across the floor using her remaining appendages; wet, mechanical entrails dragged behind. He watched with disgust as she pulled herself toward the control console and manually jacked herself into the ship's mainframe. This was immediately followed by a series of chirps and screeching feedback as she tapped into the computer's audio circuitry in order to communicate.

" . . . *skritch* . . . Captain . . . *skritch* . . . Vega."

"Yes, Sona. I can hear you. What the hell's going on?"

Sona made more audio adjustments, and the next time she spoke her voice had been equalized to sound more or less human.

"An HH slipped through screening. It's on board and has taken a passenger. It attempted to terminate me, but didn't factor in my reserve systems."

Vega felt as if an invisible fist had slugged him in the

gut. It was the worst possible news—the worst goddamned scenario.

"Have you woken any other crew members?"

Sona's mouth moved silently, followed by a delayed voice piped through the ship's system. "No, sir. According to Directive 222A, the Captain is first to be-"

"Okay, Okay—good. Let's keep it that way. "You have my gear?

Sona gestured toward a nearby hover-cart, which contained standard issue battle armor and a loaded disrupter.

Vega reached for the sleek-looking weapon and felt the cool metal in his hand; it weighed heavy in his grip.

"There is something else, sir. Something you need to know."

He adjusted the setting on the disrupter "I know, Sona. And I'm sorry . . . "

Sona's face exploded from a direct shot to the head. A delayed high-pitched screech emanated from the ship's computer a moment later—then stopped abruptly.

Vega set the weapon—still humming from the discharge—back on the cart and began to put on his armor. He would deal with Sona's remains and alter the ship's records later. There was a more pressing matter at hand.

∼∼

Vega moved stealthily up several flights of stairs toward the Crew Deck. The ship's security system had logged some recent movement in the Mess Hall. The turbolift wasn't an option; the noise would give him away. He would need the advantage of surprise if he was to have any hope of taking down an HH in close quarters.

As he crept toward the main entrance to the Crew

Deck, he double-checked his weapon. At its highest setting, the disrupter emitted a lethal blast of concentrated microwave and UV radiation. But that was cold comfort; the creature's speed, strength, and ferocity gave it an enormous edge.

He moved as quietly as possible through the silent Mess Hall. The hundred or so empty chairs gave the large room an eerie quality. Memories of his crewmates eating there flashed in his mind and he longed for their company. Vega had never been good at being alone and the sense of isolation he felt now was almost unbearable.

He forced thoughts of his crew away and continued toward the entertainment area of the Mess Hall. It was both absurd and perverse to imagine a HH needing entertainment, and yet, it made sense that he might find it here. After all, what else would it do once the eating had been taken care of? There was nothing to do on the ship but eat, shit and sleep.

Vega scanned the area, his weapon held in firing position.

Nothing.

He spun in all directions, prepared to annihilate anything that moved, when something caught his eye.

As he looked closer he noticed brightly colored images moving on a holo-screen. It was an episode of the popular cartoon *Gloop and Gloopy*. The sound was muted, though, and the room was as still as a mausoleum.

Tentatively, he moved closer, his jaw clenched so tightly his teeth began to ache. The tunic beneath his battle armor was drenched in sweat, his heart felt as if it were about to burst through his chest plate.

A faint rasping sound.

It seemed to emanate from the other side of a black

lounger just ahead—a large one that probably sat twelve comfortably. From Vega's vantage point—looking at the back of it—no one appeared to be sitting there.

He switched to a two-handed grip and rushed toward it, finger tight on the weapon's trigger.

What he saw caught him by surprise. Sprawled out on the floor was a teenage girl; she was a brunette with a boyish figure—perhaps 14 years old. Her standard-issue uniform was still intact and she appeared completely unharmed.

Her chest rose and fell ever so slightly, and there was a slight rasp to her breath. *She's still in stasis*, he thought. She'd been taken from her sleep pod without being awakened. It would take a special chemical injection to bring her back to consciousness.

There were two types of HH victims: "Transmitters" and "Feeders." Transmitters were human hosts used to propagate the parasites; Feeders were humans used solely as sustenance. HH was an abbreviation for 'Homo Hirudinea,' a scientific term for the human host of a parasitic alien. Earth's general populace, of course, chose more colorful terms, such as 'Leeches,' 'Hemo-Gobblers,' 'Vamps,' and 'BFTs' (Big Fucking Ticks).

Once a victim was infected, chemical changes to their hormones, along with a massive overproduction of adrenaline, resulted in superhuman strength and reflexes. Muscle, bone and connective tissue thickened, followed by functional changes to the teeth and nails—presumably for capturing prey. Inexplicably, the transformation made the host extremely vulnerable to the ultra violet spectrum while producing an insatiable desire for human hemotophagy— feeding on human blood. For these reasons, many believed that scouting missions by the parasites early in mankind's history had originated the vampire myth.

Vega's grip on his disrupter tightened.

A shadow passed over the girl's face.

It's above us, Vega thought. *Clinging to the ceiling.*

The HH landed on him, using the same terrible claws on his helmet that it had used to climb the walls.

Before he could get off a shot, it had ripped the disrupter from his hand and torn off his faceplate with inhuman strength. Vega scrunched his eyes shut, anticipating the worst: he would either be sucked dry or turned. He hoped it was the former.

But the bite didn't come.

He could smell fetid breath on his face. And something wet dripped onto his cheek, sliding down past his neck. *Saliva? Blood?*

Both?

When he could no longer bear the waiting he opened his eyes. Inches from his face the creature gazed at him. The first thing Vega noticed was its teeth. They were sharp all right, but they were still small and hadn't fully formed yet.

Its features were angelic, with the supple skin of a seven-year-old boy.

The eyes were haunted, but familiar.

"Hello, son," Vega choked.

And then, deep within those icy blue eyes, Vega saw a hint of recognition. They began to soften. And he knew at that moment that his son had not completely turned.

"It's me, Arrycc. It's Daddy."

The boy's face trembled and tears welled in his eyes. His mouth began to quiver, as if trying to remember how to speak.

And then a word came that Vega didn't think he would ever hear again.

"Daddy?"

There was confusion on the boy's face, as if he'd woken

from a deep coma and was struggling to put together the fragments of his memories.

"It's me, little monkey," Vega said, a term of endearment he'd used since his son was a baby.

It was as if a dam broke inside the boy. Tears gushed and he threw his arms around his father as if he'd been away for years. And technically, he had.

Vega reached up and tried to hug his son as best he could while wearing battle armor. "It's okay. I'm here now. It's okay."

He held his son for a long time, feeling the boy's moist face against his.

Soon the reality of the situation began to sink in. Arrycc's intended victim only a few feet away from them. The parasite inside his son. His own treachery to get the boy onboard the ship.

They stood up and faced each other awkwardly. The boy averted his eyes from the girl, ashamed. Vega glanced down and sighed with relief.

He hasn't turned all the way. Maybe I can still save him.

⁓

The origin of the parasites had been impossible to authenticate, but many in the scientific community speculated they were interdimensional. At a quantum level they vibrated at a frequency that made them imperceptible to the naked eye—until they possessed a human host.

The epidemic had been as fast as it was complete; spreading to every human-occupied mining colony, outpost and space station. Physicists speculated that the invaders utilized some form of quantum tunneling technology, enabling them to travel through the multiverse in ways far beyond our scientific capabilities.

Zeta-12, a deep space research station was the only remaining outpost that survived the invasion. The team there, led by Dr. Mirann Tael, was renowned for their groundbreaking work in genetic engineering, specifically in immunology. Their greatest triumph was "'Batch 779,'" a prototype biotech curative that combined nanotechnology with alien plant DNA.

Batch 779 had been engineered to enhance the immune system and protect against a myriad of diseases; early human trials had showed great promise. During the parasite invasion, it was discovered that Batch 779 had an added benefit; it provided resistance to the parasites. And while the curative had saved the lives of the Zeta-12 crew, without any way to mass-produce it, or transport it quickly enough, it had been too late to save Earth or its interstellar colonies.

Vega and the passengers of his ship, *the Phoenix*, were currently on a course for Zeta-12, to get Batch 779 inoculations. Vega had put his son in stasis with the intention of getting him the curative before the parasite turned him completely. And the plan would have worked if the boy hadn't awoken early, six months before reaching their destination.

Vega tried to convince Arrycc to return to his sleep pod with the promise of a cure. He first appealed to him with reason, then begged and pleaded, and later threatened the boy. But Arrycc refused, clearly under the influence of the parasite. Back on ORION, the space station closest to Earth, his son had been bitten less than twenty-four hours before going into stasis on *the Phoenix*. However, according to Sona's daily logs, the boy woke eight hours before Vega had. This meant that technically—not counting the five years they had been in stasis—his son had been infected for four days. The incubation period was approximately a week.

During the first few days, victims would generally maintain some semblance of their original identity. But inevitably they would succumb to the parasite's influence and become what some crudely referred to as 'walking meat puppets.'

How Arrycc had awoken from stasis was still a mystery. He could only assume that the physiology of the parasite, which was completely alien in nature, gave it some sort of resistance to the stasis field. The thought of how far they had come, how much they had been through, only to lose the battle now—was almost too much to bear. The parasite epidemic had destroyed everything Vega had ever known or cared about, his best friend Tallic, his little sister Norra, and his wife Ahn.

ORION had been ill prepared for the parasite invasion, their armory woefully inadequate. The Earth Defense Network discovered, quite by accident, that the parasites were vulnerable to microwave and UV radiation. Once word got to ORION of the parasite's weakness, they had retrofitted as much weaponry as they could, but there simply hadn't been enough time to battle the parasites effectively.

Vega was the captain of *the Phoenix*, the only interstellar ship docked at ORION at the time of the attack. As the highest ranking military officer on the station, he was forced to make difficult decisions, such as initiating a lottery to decide who would gain access to *the Phoenix*, and who would have to stay behind.

Some of the lottery winners were immediately disqualified, as blood samples revealed that they had already been infected. Vega used his power and influence to sneak Arrycc on board the ship and bypass the screening process altogether.

It had been a long shot to save his son, and he'd risked everything for it; his crew, the passengers—even himself. If his plan were discovered, he would face a court martial and most likely, the death penalty. But it was a risk he was willing to take. Arrycc was all he had left to live for.

Humankind's survival had been foremost on Vega's mind since he'd awoken. Between his passengers, crew and the 74 inhabitants of Zeta-12—there were 574 human beings that represented the remainder of humanity.

From 10,000,000,000 to 574 in the span of a year—it was still unfathomable.

And yet there was hope. The terraformed planet on which Zeta-12 stood was in its final phase; and according to Dr. Tael, it was capable of sustaining the passengers and crew of *the Phoenix* for a lifetime.

There was one small problem.

Arrycc.

Vega realized, with growing dread, that if he didn't get his son back into hyper sleep soon, he would have no choice but to kill him.

~~~

He found Arrycc in the same place as before, sitting entranced in front of the holo-screen. He moved a few steps toward his son, who sniffed at the air absently, and then went back to watching the screen.

It was *Gloop and Gloopy* again, Arrycc's favorite show since as far back as Vega could remember. It revolved around the misadventures of two teenage aliens who had crash-landed on Earth after taking their dad's spaceship for a joyride.

Vega stood there for a long moment, staring at his boy, longing to hold him. A swarm of memories surged up all at once. The first was of the day he'd been carrying his infant son, and the naked boy had taken a poop—right in
~~~

his hand. Vega cried out to his wife for help, but Ahn was too busy crumpled on the floor with laughter.

He smiled at the memory.

Next, he remembered the first time Arrycc had ridden a hover-board by himself, and the pride he'd felt watching his boy soar. He recalled reading to Arrycc before bedtime, who would beg him for old stories of ghosts and goblins and things that go bump in the night. Afterward, he would have to promise that the monsters weren't real.

And now his son was becoming one.

Two days prior, when Vega thought Arrycc had turned, he'd been prepared to kill him. But now, as he stood in the doorway, watching his own flesh and blood, he knew he couldn't—not if there was the slightest chance he could save him.

He entered the room and made his way to the lounger. As he sat next to Arrycc, his body tensed. The boy revealed no emotion; it was all the more eerie listening to the cartoon's canned laugh track.

They sat in silence for an uncomfortably long time. At first it seemed like a perverse joke, a dark and twisted mockery of times past, when they'd huddled together in front of the holo-screen. All they needed now was a bucket of popcorn and a bucket of blood to wash it down.

However, as the hours passed, Vega's revulsion began to pass. The desperate need to connect with his son was like a silent third party. Sitting there, he could almost pretend that things were normal. He could even imagine his wife, Ahn, off in the kitchen making one of her amazing dishes.

When the longing became too much to bear, he reached around his son's shoulders; it was as if he was watching from outside himself—not completely in control of his actions.

His son glanced at him for a moment. Deep within those sunken eyes, there appeared to be a spark of humanity.

It was enough.

Vega didn't move for some time, afraid that any motion might disturb the boy and shatter the illusion.

Arrycc didn't move either.

Vega knew that at any point the boy could turn, literally and figuratively. But something about the look they'd shared told him he wasn't in danger.

Not yet.

How long would their father-son bond protect him? The amount of time it took to succumb to a parasite's influence varied from person to person. He had heard of extreme cases on Earth where particularly strong-willed individuals managed to retain their identity for several weeks.

Arrycc certainly had a strong will going for him, something he'd inherited from both his parents. And, of course, the boy's love for him had always been strong. But how long would love and the will of a seven-year-old boy last?

The hunger was inevitable.

For now he wouldn't think about it. For now he would cherish what might be their final moments together.

∿

The hunger came.

Four days later he found Arrycc in the stasis chamber with a new victim, dragging a teenage boy with thick red hair from his sleep pod. The boy was unaware of what was happening and would remain that way unless chemically induced to consciousness.

It was a blessing.

The look on Arrycc's face was one of defiance, a look with which Vega was intimately familiar. Without his disrupter or armor he posed no threat—Arrycc could dispatch him easily.

"Arrycc," he heard himself say. It sounded rather weak, with a hint of despair. "Please . . . don't."

His son looked at him quizzically.

"Please . . . "

And then the expression on Arrycc's face seemed to melt into something else. Vega had seen it many times before, whenever his son wanted something desperately, like a brand new toy or an extra helping of dessert.

He had always had a hard time saying no to him. Ahn had often teased him about it. *How can a man used to ordering around a crew all day have such a hard time saying no to a little boy?*

But they had both known the answer. Vega's career kept him from his family so much that he wanted to make sure he gave his son whatever he wanted when he was around. Grimly, he realized that the past week had been the longest stretch of time he'd ever spent with his son at one time.

And now, when saying "no" was the most important thing he could do, he knew it would do no good. Arrycc had the hunger now. He could see it in his eyes. God help him, there was nothing to do now but let his son feed.

Vega turned and walked away. He couldn't stop the boy from his first kill, but he sure as hell wouldn't stand around and watch.

He had barely taken a step when the grisly sounds of flesh being torn and the lapping of blood began.

~

The first death was the hardest for Vega to stomach. But as

the long weeks turned into longer months, the guilt that gnawed at him began to dissipate. Like most horrible things, prolonged exposure deadened the effects.

By the third month he had lost count of the bodies. *Was it 16 . . . 18?*

Once the victims' bodies were drained of blood, Vega dutifully jettisoned the remains into space through the garbage chute, standard protocol for corpses in deep space.

The missing passengers would have to be accounted for at some point, but he'd already worked out an explanation. He would blame their deaths on Sona. Droids weren't perfect, and breakdowns weren't unheard of. A simple miscalculation in cryo-fluids from the ship's droid would explain the passengers' deaths easily enough.

No one would suspect foul play from a twice-decorated captain with a spotless military record. Besides, survival would be first and foremost on everyone's mind once they reached the outpost.

How he would deal with Arrycc was a bit more complicated. He figured there were three ways it could go. The first option was that Arrycc would kill him. The second, he would kill his son. Third, and the least likely, he would find a way to keep Arrycc hidden while they docked at Zeta-12, just long enough to get his hands on Batch 779 and save him.

He was still trying to work out the last option. But it wasn't easy with such an unpredictable variable as the parasite.

It had now been over four months since he and his son had awoken. Arrycc was, for all intents and purposes, a bloodsucking monster. And yet, the boy's disposition had hardly changed. He had stopped speaking, of course, but that was typical. The parasites were able to communicate with each other without speaking, most likely telepathically, although that had never been proven. It was possible for them to speak through their human hosts, though rarely seen—victims of the parasites tended to simply grunt or snarl.

When Arrycc wasn't feeding or sleeping, he spent his time watching old movies and documentaries or reading through endless archives about Earth—on every conceivable topic. The sophistication level of his research had grown exponentially in all areas of math, science and the arts. He seemed to especially enjoy reading about world religions and theology.

Was there any shred of Arrycc left? Vega had convinced himself there was. Why else had he been allowed to live? Of course, he was a critical member of the crew. Arrycc certainly couldn't navigate the ship by himself. But Vega clung to the former idea like a life raft, hoping Arrycc was still somewhere inside the silent figure that had become his only companion.

Arrycc didn't appear to mind Vega's presence. They would often sit next to each other in the entertainment room, watching the holo-screen. For hours they would sit quietly, often viewing documentaries, which seemed to be Arrycc's favorite.

Vega found it comforting to sit next to his son. In his mind he could almost pretend that everything was still normal. Sometimes he thought he could spend the rest of his life like this, just he and his son, spending quality time together—the kind of time he'd never had a chance to experience on the space station. He realized that if he never awoke the rest of the crew, there would be enough food to last him a lifetime.

But Arrycc would only last about five years, factoring

in the rate at which he fed on the bodies in the stasis chamber. If he had been a full-grown adult it would have been half the time . . .

The only chance his son had now was to get him to Zeta-12 and pray that Batch 779 would still work on someone this far along in the transformation process.

〰

Vega had never been so happy to see and speak to another human being in his life. If he could have reached through the communication screen he would have hugged Dr. Tael.

Now less than 24 hours away from docking at Zeta-12, they had finally reached sub space communication range. Tael was an attractive looking woman in her late sixties. She had already gone over their standard quarantine protocols, and Vega had agreed to keep his passengers onboard until proper inoculations were dispensed. No one would be allowed to enter Zeta-12 until they had been screened and cleared.

Eventually the conversation turned from strictly business to more personal issues. "How are you holding up, Captain? You don't look well."

Vega felt self-conscious, realizing at that moment how much he'd let himself go during the past six months. He'd done nothing but eat and sit with Arrycc when he could. He'd gained twenty pounds easy, and despite shaving that morning for the first time in half a year, the perpetual sleep deprivation, constant worry, and lack of any physical activity had taken its toll. He looked like hell, and he knew it.

"I haven't slept well these past few months," Vega said. That part was true. Then the lies began as he interweaved the threads of a true story he'd heard about back in his Academy days. "We had a serious droid malfunction—total systems failure. She made some miscalculations on some of the passengers' cryo-fluid levels. We lost 24 people. The backup systems woke me up before anyone else died."

Tael looked shocked. "That's terrible news, Captain. I'm so sorry. Every life is precious—now so more than ever. When did this happen?"

"A few months ago . . . goddamned droid was in full meltdown when I woke up—had to take her down with a disrupter. As if things hadn't been bad enough before . . . " He rubbed his face with his hands dramatically.

"And you never went back into stasis," Tael said. It was more of a statement than a question.

"I figured, what's the point? I knew we'd reach you in a few months."

Tael's brow furrowed at that. "Being alone on that ship, with no one to communicate with—you know the risks as well as I do."

Vega was well aware. 'Solipsism Syndrome' was a serious risk for anyone who spent long periods alone in space. It created the overwhelming feeling that nothing was real—or simply a dream. Sufferers had been known to feel so lonely and detached from the world they became utterly, and terribly indifferent.

But he wasn't alone was he? He still had his son. And he certainly wasn't losing his mind. He was just weary and emotionally drained. Who the hell wouldn't be after all he'd been through since the invasion?

"I appreciate the concern, Doc. But I'm going to wake my crew in less than 24 hours—once we're in navigation range."

Tael seemed to accept this answer and nodded politely. "I look forward to seeing you, your crew and passengers soon."

After a few more pleasantries Tael signed off.

Within a day Vega was going to have to wake his crew. He had no choice but to make a decision about his son.

He sat there for a long time collecting his thoughts . . . and his nerve.

He found Arrycc a few hours later, sitting rigidly, staring blankly at the holo-screen; his face was drenched in fresh blood. Vega was reminded of a time when Arrycc—who was two years old at the time—had buried his face into his bowl and covered it with tomato sauce. It was a sweet memory that was now twisted forever in his mind.

In Arrycc's hands was the gouged and glistening head of his latest victim. Curled under his feet like a human footstool was the body it had once been attached to. He was watching a movie and holding the head as if it were a bucket of popcorn. As Vega stepped closer, he recognized the face of the teenage girl. She was the one he'd saved from Arrycc all those months ago. Her eyes were wide open now and staring up at the face of her killer.

The boy didn't acknowledge the presence of his father. Vega did his best to ignore the blood pooled around Arrycc on the lounger as he sat down. On the screen were images from ancient Jerusalem and a man nailed to a cross.

A vampire watching a documentary about Christianity . . .

After a protracted, awkward silence, Vega said, "I have to wake my crew in a few hours. We'll be at the Zeta-12 outpost by this time tomorrow."

The boy said nothing. He stared at the images on the holo-screen with a look of bemusement. It was the first hint of emotion Vega had seen on his son's face since as far back as he could remember.

"Arrycc, listen. I can't help you . . . cure you . . . unless you work with me. We have to talk. Figure this out—now."

A grin appeared on the boy's face.

Vega slammed his fist against the lounger. "Goddamnit, Arrycc I'm talking to you!"

The boy turned toward him slowly and began to speak; it was like a winter grave had opened—cold, moist and dark.

"There is . . . no . . . Arrycc . . . here."

Vega recoiled at the voice that sounded only partially human. It appeared to be a great effort for the boy to speak, as if he were learning to use his vocal chords all over again.

"Such . . . a . . . primitive . . . way to communicate."

Vega stifled the impulse to scream. He was accustomed to his silent son, had fooled himself into thinking that he was still reachable. But the voice emanating from the boy brought a hideous new reality crashing down.

Arrycc turned back toward the holo-screen. "Your . . . religious wars fascinate me."

Vega could think of nothing to say.

"You have killed each other by the millions . . . because you don't agree about what happens to you . . . after you kill each other."

Vega stared at him, mouth agape.

"Your mind is full of questions."

Vega gave a deep sigh. *Yes.*

The boy turned toward Vega and placed a small hand against his cheek; the tiny frigid fingers pulsed with a strength that unnerved him.

Suddenly, what felt like an invisible icepick lanced Vega's brain; his body went numb. With great effort he tried to remove his son's hand, but to his horror, discovered he couldn't move.

A presence entered his mind . . . invading his thoughts, violating him.

Images flooded his mind. No . . . not images, more like tangible memories . . . memories that weren't his. They were alien, in the truest sense of the word.

He was back on Earth. He could see, taste it. Smell it. But the experience wasn't nostalgic. It was terrible . . . it was . . . *God, no . . .*

It was the end of everything.

Why? Vega's mind pleaded. *Why us?*

The question had lain dormant in him—gnawed at him, from the beginning.

Somewhere beyond the alien thoughts, he felt something familiar. A comforting presence. Pure. Innocent.

Of course . . . it was his son!

I won't let it hurt you, Daddy.

Was that a thought . . . or a feeling? Vega couldn't tell. But it was Arrycc all right. Some small part of him still alive . . . still fighting . . . still loving his father.

Vega reached for him in his mind. Goddamnit, *he* was the one who should be comforting his son. *He* was the one who should be the protector, not the other way around.

I'm sorry, Daddy.

The voice seemed to come from deep within, as if beneath a great body of water. It repeated the same thing over and over—*I'm sorry, Daddy. I'm sorry, Daddy*—the voice sinking deeper into an ocean of nothingness.

At that moment Vega knew—he was only alive because his son's love had been stronger than the parasite. And the final gift he offered his father were answers to the questions that had haunted him since the start of the invasion.

The information came all at once like a quantum speed

download. But they weren't thoughts as normally processed by the brain. This was experiential. His mind was not his own anymore. He was experiencing the past through the prism of an alien intelligence.

No longer was he in the known universe—it was another dimension of time and space. He was one of them now. There was no English translation for their name; the most appropriate word his mind could grasp was . . . *Legion*.

They were more sophisticated than anything he could imagine, yet like all living organisms, they required sustenance. As interdimensional predators their mission was simple: eat and reproduce.

The Legion that invaded Earth was a tiny fraction of their race's immeasurable size—yet they had consumed the human population in a matter of months. It was the way of the Legion, an event called *the Feeding* that took place once every few million years.

At the end of the Legion's feeding and reproductive cycle, they would withdraw from the reaped world and return to their interdimensional limbo, where they would hibernate—until it was again time for the Feeding.

But that wasn't the true horror of the Legion. They were also a highly advanced race of engineers that created life to sustain their great hunger throughout the multiverse. They seeded planets and gave them time to develop and grow, returning millions of years later for the harvest.

Earth was only one of these worlds.

It had been seeded by the Legion with hominids genetically cultivated to evolve and populate the planet.

Vega screamed in his mind, desperate to break contact with the information stream. He feared his sanity was starting to slip.

It couldn't be! The Legion had created humanity and nearly destroyed it. They were our gods *and* our devils.

Something snapped then, like an invisible tether, and the telepathic link was disconnected. Vega immediately regained control over his thoughts and his body again.

His eyes snapped open and he recoiled at the face of his son, whose nose was only inches from his. The curves of his smile had barbs to the edges.

"I know you have a disruptor hidden on you," said the ghastly thing within his son's body. "But you won't use it. You love him too much."

Arrycc's head exploded outward in a fine red spray, showering Vega with his own flesh and blood.

"You're right . . . " said Vega. " . . . I love him too much."

He tossed the disruptor, still warm from its discharge, across the room.

He collapsed onto the destroyed body of his son and allowed himself to weep. It grew into a horrific wail as the terrible grieving he'd kept bottled up inside finally came pouring out.

~

Vega spent several hours cleaning up the remains of his son's body before awakening a handful of essential crewmembers. The landing preparations and briefing of his most senior staff were welcome distractions. When he brought up the tragedy of losing 26 passengers, he had shed real tears; the fact that his son had been amongst the victims went a long way toward avoiding suspicion.

Docking at Zeta-12 had gone like clockwork. Dr. Tael, along with two very attractive lab assistants, had been gracious, accommodating, and had screened the crew of *the*

Phoenix with diplomacy and grace. Once the screenings were completed and the landing party of ten had been cleared, Tael gave them a tour of the impressive facility. According to Tael's calculations, their terraforming work was nearly complete.

That evening, a feast for Vega and his crew was prepared; it was a celebration of their survival and the human race.

Vega was grateful. Tael and her team's hospitality, empathy and optimism had gone a long way toward lifting the somber spirits of the crew. He actually heard Sygar, his science officer, laugh at a joke Kentol, the communications officer, had made. Sygar retold the joke and sent the whole crew into gales of laughter. The joke wasn't really that funny, but in times of great stress, laughter was like a release valve—once it was opened, it came in an unstoppable flood.

When the laughter had finally subsided, Vega felt light-headed. He couldn't remember the last time he had laughed that hard. He felt positively giddy. As he looked around at his crew, he noticed they all had odd, silly expressions on their faces. If he didn't know any better, he'd have sworn they all looked . . .

Drugged.

That was Vega's last thought before the darkness consumed him.

~

"Wake up, Captain Vega. They want you awake when they feed."

Vega's eyes fluttered open. He was strapped to a gurney and gazing into the cold eyes of Dr. Tael.

The gray-haired woman offered a perverse grin. "Apparently, adrenaline makes our blood taste that much sweeter."

Vega had been stripped naked and was covered with a thin, bloodstained sheet. He struggled futilely against his bindings. Within minutes his gurney was being pushed through a long, narrow passageway. The lighting was sparse, casting everything in shadow. They appeared to be in the lower levels of Zeta-12, probably somewhere in the storage area.

Tael was walking along the right side of him tapping notes into a com-pad. Vega glanced up to see a fresh-faced woman with lovely hair and a perfectly shaped nose looking down at him as she pushed the gurney through the murkiness. One of Tael's lab assistants—Myris was her name?

It had been impossible to keep all of their names straight; the Zeta-12 crew was over 70 strong. He suddenly recalled a term he'd heard from stories back on Earth: 'Familiars'. They were a lesser known, but essential part of ancient vampire lore. Like so many facets of vampire legend that had originated with the Legion, they had proved to be true. Familiars were humans who worked with vampires but had not yet been turned; they were useful because of their ability to walk in the daylight and do the dirty work of their masters.

Some familiars were controlled psychically, while others had personal reasons for their service; the promise of power and immortality were irresistible to some.

Zeta-12 had never been humankind's last hope—it was to be its final stop. His crew had been doomed from the day they left ORION. There had never been a cure, of that he was convinced. It had been a lure to get the very last of them—the Legion didn't leave survivors.

The gurney stopped abruptly. Tael entered a code into a control interface built into the wall. A moment later, a dull metal door slid open, and the foul odor that wafted out made Vega gag. Neither Tael nor her assistant seemed to be bothered.

"I'll take it from here." Tael said to the blonde, who glanced down at Vega, offering a smile devoid of warmth. "Goodbye," she said.

A space station populated with familiars, Vega thought. His crew never stood a chance.

He had heard stories about familiars—or people like them—back on Earth during the invasion; some were high-ranking government officials and military officers that had helped the vamps during several critical stages of the war.

What had they been promised? Power? Immortality? Whatever the case, the joke had been on them—eventually they had fared no better than the rest of humanity.

He felt a jerk as he was pulled into the shadows of a sizable room, the metal creaking of his gurney echoing eerily. The only illumination in the stench-filled space was ambient light from the passageway.

"I'm afraid this is where we part ways," said Tael. "Take some comfort in knowing that you'll join us in service to our Alpha."

"Alpha?" Vega said, and his teeth chattered as he said it.

"The leader of our little group."

Vega grunted in acknowledgment.

Tael locked the wheels of the gurney and started to leave.

Vega called out. "Can I ask you something?"

"Yes?"

"What did this . . . *Alpha* promise you?"

Tael hesitated for a moment and then said, "The survival of our species."

Vega had to laugh. "Well then, Doc . . . I guess the joke's on all of us."

"Really."

"Yeah. See . . . there's this one little thing they probably didn't tell you."

The stone-faced woman stepped closer, suddenly interested in what Vega had to say.

"We're not the first ones to populate Earth," Vega said with gritted teeth. "And we won't be the last."

Tael's face was hidden in the darkness, but her silence spoke volumes.

"You would've been better off developing a *real* cure, Doc. Once the feeding is over, they'll wipe the slate clean and press the reset button."

Tael began to walk away.

Vega called out with a vengeful laugh, "You're going to vanish like you never existed . . . you just don't know it yet!"

"We'll see," Tael said with a slight waver right before the heavy door closed behind her.

Vega grinned in the darkness. That had given him a modicum of satisfaction. He could hear Tael's footsteps resonating through the empty passageway beyond the door. Once they faded, all he could hear was his own heavy breathing.

Or was that all?

He listened closer. Something else was in the room.

It had been waiting.

It moved. And what he heard next sounded like the gnashing of enormous teeth.

As his eyes began to adjust to the darkness he noticed something hanging above him; it was immense in size and staring right at him. Its twelve eyes had a pulsing luminance.

With slow deliberation, it lowered its hideous, misshapen body toward him. It looked like five or six people fused together somehow, as if one human body wasn't enough to contain it. And inside its gaping maw were rows of needle-sharp teeth, seeming to jostle and compete with each other.

Vega closed his eyes.

He thought of the ten billion or so that had been erased from existence and wondered about the meaning of it all. He dove deeper into the shadowy maze of his mind, searching . . . and when he had finally reached what felt like the bottom of an abyss, he found what he was looking for. It was warm and familiar, a comforting feeling that came from thoughts of his wife and son.

Perhaps love had been the point after all.

Maybe next time, he thought, humanity will get it right.

Dead Pull

EVERY ANIMAL FELL silent the moment Brennan stepped inside the pet store. A modest brass bell above the door clanged dully.

He surveyed his animal kingdom; satisfied with the respect his subjects paid him. It bordered on reverence, which, Brennan felt, was fully his due. Four Dachshund puppies stopped their play fighting and slinked back to the corners of their cage. A handful of kittens leapt behind their scratching posts and into the hollows of barrels and other playthings. The tropical birds watched him intently, none daring to caw. Even the rodents and the fish had stopped all activity, as if they sensed a storm gathering on the horizon.

The insects didn't seem to notice Brennan, but of course he realized they were too stupid to know any better. He was still working on that.

Fear pervaded the store, strong enough to taste.

Brennan was pleased.

He began his morning routine by flicking on the store lights, followed by checking the bills and coinage in the register drawer. He was compelled to recount it in the mornings because the two dipsticks on the night shift couldn't count past ten without a goddamn calculator. They shortchanged him more often than not, no matter how many times he'd complained to the owner.

Animals, Brennan had discovered, were far easier to teach and control than people. Unfortunately, he couldn't get away with conditioning people as easily as animals. Control was what Brennan desired; lack of it had blazed a trail of disaster throughout his life: alcoholism, failed career ambitions, a monumentally disastrous marriage, and a body that increasingly tipped the wrong side of the scale.

Brennan was startled when the phone rang, shattering the silence of the store. He glanced at the kitschy wall clock that was made to look like an owl, its eyes clicking side to side as the pendulum swung.

It was exactly 7:59am.

He pondered whether or not to answer the phone. After all, the store wasn't officially open for business for a full sixty seconds.

On the tenth ring, he gave an annoyed huff and answered it. "Purrs, Grrs and Furs, the happy pet store," delivered deadpan with the word 'store' warped to rhyme with 'fur'.

A husky voice on the other end of the line said, "It's me, Brennan. I meant to leave ya a note, but I forgot."

It was Guthrie, the storeowner.

Brennan did his best to sound perky, never an easy task. "Morning. What's up?"

"I meant to tell ya last week. I approved a work internship for Ed Mackey's kid, Billy. He's gonna shadow ya today. He'll be working with us through the summer for school credit—Monday through Friday."

Brennan felt his face flush. "Listen, I don't-"

Guthrie cut him off, "I know ya like to work alone, Brenn. But Mackey's an important customer. I met his kid and he's sharp. Wants to be a freakin' zoologist, specializin' in fish or some such, ain't that a kicker?"

Christ, that's all I need, Brennan thought, *some little smart ass rambling on all day about the finer points of goldfish reproduction.* Between gritted teeth, he replied, "I guess I don't have much choice."

Guthrie cleared his throat. "Hell, me neither. Mackey spends more money on them exotic fish than you earn in a whole year. What would ya do in my position?"

Brennan didn't have anything to say that wouldn't get him fired.

"It's all settled then," Guthrie said. "Stay on your best behavior now. I know how territorial you can get."

The moment Brennan heard the dial tone he flung the phone across the counter. It hit the tile floor with a jarring *clang*. One of the tropical birds in the back gave a startled squawk.

"Shut up, goddamnit!" Brennan shouted at the bird.

The store went deathly quiet.

A moment later Billy Mackey knocked on the front door.

~~~

The boy spun through the store like an ambitious cyclone. He stocked more shelves in the first hour than Brennan normally did in two days. By hour three he'd completely reorganized the amphibian section and was tackling a cat food display in earnest.

Brennan's sufferance ended abruptly. He grasped the boy's shoulder firmly and said, "Listen up, Rookie. It's time for the dead pull."

Mackey gave Brennan a confused look. "Dead pull?"

"Sure. Loads of fun."

Mackey put the finishing touches to the cat food display, and then raced through the aisles to catch up with Brennan.
~~~

The store was claustrophobic, overflowing with every conceivable—and some inconceivable—pet need.

Brennan noted that the animals seemed to take a great interest in the teenaged boy. Several puppies and cats came out of hiding for the first time since Brennan had stepped into the store. The youngest Yorkshire Terrier gave a yip or two and tried to catch Mackey's attention, his tail wagging wildly as his paws scratched against the thick plastic of his cage. Brennan made a mental note to teach the little furry bastard a lesson about scratching at his cage.

When they moved past the bird section, the largest Congo African Grey gave a mighty squawk and two small lovebirds cooed. Brennan ground his teeth, saying nothing, his face deepening to a fierce red. He suddenly realized he would have to constantly keep his anger in check with Mackey around. The little cocksucker's prying eyes would be on him five days a week.

But not for long if I can help it.

As they entered the aquatics section, Brennan flicked on the special aquarium lights, illuminating an array of native and exotic fish. Dashes of brilliant color darted through the water.

Mackey was immediately drawn to a particular freshwater tank.

With an intensity that belied his age, he said, "Has anyone checked the PH and ammonia in this tank?"

Brennan busied himself with two tangled fishnets, refusing to justify the boy's question.

Mackey studied a school of luminous Neon Tetras. "These Tetras are developing some 'Ich'. You see those white spots?"

Brennan's temper rose. "I know what Ich is, Rookie."

Mackey immediately caught Brennan's tone and realized

that he'd overstepped his bounds. He pulled in his head like a scared turtle. "Right . . . right, of course."

Brennan tossed him a small net and pointed to three plastic buckets on the floor; one marked "Freshwater," the other "Saltwater" and the last "Feeder." All were filled with chemically treated water.

"Don't mix the nets," he growled. "It taints the water and spreads disease."

Brennan knew the kid was fully aware of this. Hell, his family was a bunch of fish freaks. But it felt good to reinforce his authority. It also pleased him to watch Mackey biting his tongue, wanting to shout: *I know all of this*! Apparently, the little shit was smart enough to keep his mouth shut.

Brennan reiterated, "Take special care to keep the feeder nets separate. They're the worst carriers of bacteria. You got that?"

"Got it."

"Good." Brennan pointed at a wooden clipboard hanging on the wall. "Right here's the dead pull list. It has to be filled out every morning."

"You mean . . . as in pull out the dead ones?"

"You catch on quick, Rookie."

Mackey shifted on his feet, apprehensive. "Are there usually a lot of dead ones?"

"Welcome to the glamour of pet retail, Pal."

Mackey's face deflated as if it had sprung a leak, which gave Brennan great satisfaction.

"First, you pull all the dead ones from the tanks," Brennan said. "Then, you put 'em in those plastic baggies over there. Make sure to write the name, quantity and stock number on the dead pull list. Think you can handle that?"

"Sure. Of course," Mackey said. He seemed to be trying extra hard to keep things friendly.

Brennan remained austere. "When you're done, you can do the same thing with the reptiles and small animals."

Brennan had just finished ringing up his first customer for the day when he glanced over and saw Mackey pulling a dead, bloated rat from its cage. It was stiff as a frozen pack of meat and he knew from experience that it probably smelled even worse than it looked. He chuckled at Mackey's disgusted expression as he tried and failed to stuff the rat's long, unaccommodating tail into the small plastic baggie. The boy appeared more disheartened with each and every dead pull.

Just wait till you see what's next, Kiddo.

A few moments later, Mackey called out with genuine concern, "Some of these kittens back here are pretty sick."

"Don't sweat the 'free adoptions'," Brennan yelled back, while inserting a fresh roll of tape into the register. "They're donated."

Mackey was clearly upset by what he'd seen. "But they're ..."

"I said *forget it*. We don't pay for mongrel cats, so who gives a shit. Now come on, you've got more important work to do."

Brennan hated many things, but the basement was near the top of his lengthy list. It was poorly lit, cramped, and suffused with the stink of death. The grease-stained walls were lined with bags of rotted pet food, broken merchandise, forgotten overstock—and God knows what else. It hadn't been cleaned in years, and his boss Guthrie—who was easily the most unkempt person Brennan knew—never seemed to push the issue.

Thank God for small favors.

Brennan sure as shit wasn't going to take it on himself.

Eight bucks an hour didn't cover giving a crap. Hell, eight bucks an hour didn't cover much of anything. Besides, if the health department ever busted the store, Guthrie's fat ass would take the heat. That's why he made the big bucks.

Brennan unclipped a set of keys from his belt loop with a jangle and unlocked the basement door. It was stained black with patches of mold.

Mackey choked on a waft of putrid dust. "Man . . . it's nasty down there."

Brennan suppressed a grin as he ambled down the stairs.

He knew to breathe through his mouth. Mackey wasn't so fortunate. The rancid air caused the boy to stumble; a bagful of dead animals slipped from his grasp and dropped to the floor a few steps below. Tiny, wide-eyed goldfish sliced moisture trails into its dusty surface.

Embarrassed, the boy scrambled down the steps to pick them up. Brennan stopped him with a firm hand and said, "Screw the feeders, Rookie. We inventory those in bulk anyway."

"But they'll rot down here."

Brennan waved his hand with aplomb. "Nah. They'll get eaten by morning."

Mackey cocked his head awkwardly. "Eaten?"

"Sure. Didn't you notice all the shredded bags of pet food down here?"

Mackey swallowed audibly. "Rats?"

Brennan felt a quiet glee warm his heart watching Mackey's face grow pale. "Rats, snakes, lizards . . . you name it. Every once in a while one escapes from their cage. The damn things are impossible to catch once they end up down here. And let me tell you . . . some of those bastards have gotten pretty big."

Mackey glanced nervously at the darkened corners of the basement.

Brennan continued, "But hey, you're good with animals, right? Ain't nothin' you can't handle."

Mackey put on a brave face. "No . . . it's fine."

But they both knew it wasn't fine at all.

They reached an old wooden door at the farthest end of the basement; *Freezer Room* was stenciled across it, and again Brennan had to unlock it. As they stepped inside the musty space, the smell had become just a nose hair short of unbearable. A single light bulb flickered overhead, revealing an antiquated freezer against the back wall with an ominous strobe effect.

Brennan flipped through the keys on his impressive key ring until he found the right one, and opened the lock on the freezer door. Purposefully, he waited before opening it.

"The dead pulls go in here."

Mackey took a wary step toward the humming, rusted appliance; he looked as stiff as the tiny corpses dangling from his hands. The intensity of the smell caused him to gag a bit, though he tried to conceal it.

"You can thank the boss for the lovely aroma," Brennan said. "He's too damn cheap to replace this old bitch of a freezer. Hell, it barely stays above room temperature inside there."

Brennan stepped back from the droning apparatus and moved toward the doorway of the room. "Arrange them nice and neat in there, Rookie. Our vendor collects the dead pulls on Fridays and he's a real pain in my ass if they're not organized."

Mackey offered a pitiful nod. Brennan could see the boy's enthusiasm draining like dirty water from a bathtub.

"When you're done organizing the dead pulls," Brennan said, "sweep up this room. Then you can start on the basement. There's a broom and dustpan buried . . . I don't know, somewhere in here, and there's a box of garbage bags in that cabinet just above your head."

Mackey gazed at the walls, Brennan thought, like a first-time convict exploring the walls of his new prison cell.

Brennan smiled, but it came off more like a grimace. "Have fun, Kiddo." *You think the smell is bad now* . . .

Brennan had made it halfway up the basement stairs when he heard Mackey open the freezer door with a slow creak. The boy immediately started to dry retch.

A satisfied chuckle rose in Brennan's throat.

Mornings were always the slowest, and by 11:00am only two customers had come into the pet store: a neurotic regular who bought his cat food one freaking can at a time and an exceedingly tattooed woman wanting a leather collar with spikes. Whether it was for her dog or her own couture wasn't clear.

Brennan hadn't heard a peep from Mackey since he'd left him retching in the freezer room. He probably should have warned the kid about the door's nasty habit of swinging shut. And it might have been a good idea to make sure the doorknob wasn't locked either. But, hey . . . these things happen.

When another hour and a half passed without a sound, Brennan decided it was time to check on the brat's progress. As he stepped down into the basement, he scanned the shadows for any sign of Mackey. From the look of things, nothing had been touched.

"Hey Rookie . . . you down here?"

The room seemed to hold its breath.

Intrigued, Brennan moved toward the freezer room. Much to his delight, he noticed that the door was shut tight, locked from the outside.

"You in there, Rook?" he called out, fumbling with his keys in the gloom.

A mewling sound emanated from beyond the door, causing a field of goose bumps to spring up on Brennan's arms.

That can't be good.

As he opened the freezer room door, he half-expected to see Mackey curled in a ball, drooling and staring into the darkness like some asylum escapee.

He wasn't far off.

Mackey sat on the floor right next to the freezer, slumped forward, his body stiff and unmoving. The rusted metal door of the freezer gaped open; inside a meager bulb glowed dismally. Brennan presumed that Mackey had left the freezer door open to help illuminate the tenebrous room. Inside the icebox, a menagerie of faces offered dead stares from behind plastic veils. On the bottom shelf was a baggie filled with what looked like a frozen rodent orgy. Brennan looked into the dead, clouded-over eyes of a Siamese cat, its face congealed into a perverse grin.

He quickly averted his gaze.

Mackey's chin was touching his chest. It reminded Brennan of a picture he'd once seen in a magazine: a man gunned down by a firing squad, slumped against a blood-splattered wall.

With false concern, he said, "Hey Rook, you okay?"

The kid's body jerked at that, startling Brennan. His nostril's flared from the fusion of smells that pervaded the room. Glancing down, he noticed that the crotch of the boy's jeans was dark with urine.

A corpulent rat with filthy white fur and ugly, pinkish eyes scuttled over Mackey's legs. It gave Brennan a quick once over before stuffing its gluttonous form through a gnawed hole in the wall.

Mackey's face was wan and streaked with tears as he stared at Brennan. The knuckles on his hands were swollen, torn open and bleeding—most likely from a futile session of pounding on the door.

His eyes bored into Brennan and he choked, "I wanna . . . go home."

Brennan almost felt sorry for him.

Almost.

~~~

The next day was business as usual. Billy Mackey had been successfully traumatized, and Brennan thought it unlikely that he would ever set foot in the store again.

It had been a calculated risk, of course. The little shit could have blamed him for the incident and he might have lost his job. At the same time, he knew that the risk of working with Mackey for any length of time was far greater. It wouldn't have ended well.

These types of situations never worked out well for Brennan.

Fortunately, his gambit had paid off. He'd known it would work the moment he saw Mackey trying to conceal his urine-soaked pants. The boy's profound embarrassment would keep him from telling anyone about it. Brennan was convinced of it.

That thought gave him a profound sense of control. And the control he wielded over his life seemed to begin and end with the pet store. Working there enabled him to dictate the day-to-day operations, as well as the lives of the store's denizens. The animals answered to him. Depended on him. And, more importantly, they feared him.

Those that couldn't be controlled were killed.
~~~

Brennan preferred control to killing, but he wasn't averse to dispatching uncooperative subjects. Nor was he averse to convincing the huddled masses when necessary— just to keep them in line. He'd found that teaching by example was a powerful tool; particularly with the higher intelligence animals like cats and dogs.

Fish, of course, were the easiest to lord over. They were the most vulnerable and inherently fearful.

That is, until *it* showed up.

The special delivery package arrived exactly one week after the basement incident. It was marked 'live animals', and had come courtesy of the Mackey family. An attached card offered a well-written thank you from Billy's father to Guthrie, and an acknowledgement of Brennan's exemplary tutelage.

The card went on to explain that Billy had received a rare opportunity to work at the local zoo and would no longer be able to continue his internship at the pet store. But thanks for giving him the opportunity and won't you please accept this rare exotic fish as a token of our appreciation?

Brennan had read the card with delight, relishing the subtext. The 'opportunity' at the zoo may have been real enough, but he also knew it was the Mackey's elaborate way of saving face.

However, over the next few days, the 'gift' would become the bane of Brennan's existence. And he was determined to kill it. Unfortunately, the fish had arrived on one of Guthrie's scheduled work days (planned with great precision by the Mackey's no doubt), and Brennan wouldn't be able to dispose of the fish without raising suspicion.

Better not to do anything drastic for a week or two.

In the meantime, Brennan was forced to create a home

for the unidentified fish in the large, center aquarium. *A place of honor*, were the hopelessly fawning words Guthrie used.

The description attached to the fish's shipping crate was infuriatingly cryptic. There were no instructions or identifying information other than the fish was a rare, freshwater species that thrived best alone.

Brennan wasn't surprised. It was just like the Mackeys to show off their ability to acquire extremely exotic species, daring all and sundry to identify it. *Smug, self-important bastards*. They loved to make everyone aware of their access to all things elite.

Brennan had yet to identify the shimmering black fish a week later. Oddly, none of his usual aquatic resources could find a match. Aesthetically, he found the fish to be rather unremarkable. Its physical characteristics were an amalgamation of any number of exotic species.

But there was something about its eyes. There was a cognizance he'd never seen in a fish before. Its huge, iridescent eyes seemed to peer into his soul, and disapprove of what it saw.

Brennan was reminded of the looks his father had given him during some of his more terrifying drunken benders. He felt that same kind of hatred radiating from the fish.

He'd end those hateful looks by killing it, as he'd killed his father on his thirteenth birthday. Killing, he'd found, was often the simplest solution to a difficult situation. It had always come easily to Brennan. The hardest part was getting away with it.

His ex-wife had been a real challenge.

Yes, he'd enjoy getting rid of Little Mackey (the moniker he'd given the hateful fish), but he'd have to be extremely careful. And he obsessed about the best method for the next few days. The easiest answer was to simply add salt to the tank. The problem was that it would take a fair amount to kill the fish and he didn't want to risk anyone noticing the crusty residue.

Another option was starvation, but there was no way to keep the morons on the night shift from feeding it; especially that goddamned tree-hugger, Jenkins, who doted over fish nearly as much as Billy Mackey.

Brennan also considered using the poisoned pellets he'd developed specifically for aquatic life, but he had a feeling the damned fish wouldn't eat them. And he couldn't take the chance that the pellets might be discovered at the bottom of the tank. Jenkins, in particular, would happily rat him out.

If worse came to worst, he knew he could always go with the final option: snatch the little pecker from its tank and watch it suffocate.

He'd entertained the last idea on several occasions, but the risk of damaging the delicate fish deterred him. Not that anyone would inspect the fish for foul play, but he liked to keep his dirty work clean. He had immense pride in his ability to avoid detection. Besides, after the early joys of brute force, he'd found he wasn't nearly as satisfied nowadays as when he created more ingenious killing methods. He took this as a sign of maturation.

In any case, his decision became imperative the day he noticed a power shift happening in the aquatics section. Brennan's fish subjects stopped responding in the way to which he was accustomed.

Normally, they were reactive, hanging on his every move. His threatening gestures caused them to cower from his mighty hand and retreat to the bottom of their aquariums. Conversely, if he were playing the role of benevolent God, they would race toward the surface of the water in anticipation of their daily sustenance—thankful for the grace of the Brennan-God.

Now, they stared at him with accusatory eyes.

He thought: *It's influencing them somehow . . .*

The idea was preposterous, he knew. And yet there was no denying the abrupt change in his subjects, the condemnatory looks. Brennan had felt the same way under the chastising gaze of his father; a look that said: *you're a pathetic waste of flesh.*

"Quit staring at me!" Brennan yelled at the thousand eyes.

This seemed to increase the intensity of their gazes.

Angrily, he hurled a fish net at the center aquarium, hitting Little Mackey's tank with a dull, wet *clunk*. The raven-colored fish didn't budge. It simply floated dead center in the tank.

Defiant.

Eyes burning with hate.

Brennan looked away. He refused to have a stare down with a goddamn fish.

He'd kill it and that would be the end of it.

The next day, Brennan arrived at the store ready for the final showdown.

Little Mackey's bulbous eyes followed him with suspicion as Brennan approached its tank and angrily yanked off the lid.

"Time to die."

He angled a long, plastic spout directly over the fish and poured in a deadly mixture of food-based oil and grease he'd mixed the night before. Little Mackey darted out of the way with blinding speed and narrowly avoided the sludge.

Brennan grinned. He knew the diminutive fish was merely delaying the inevitable; there was no escape in such a confined space.

He criss-crossed the oil across the surface of the water and used a net to force it down. He watched the swirling trails of oil with great anticipation. Little Mackey continued to dodge and weave, but eventually the toxic blanket of oil coated it with a viscous sheen.

Soon the oil would clog the fragile gills of the fish, preventing it from extracting oxygen from the water. Ironically, this made Brennan breathe easier.

The ebony-colored fish would die of—what looked like—natural causes. If any suspicions arose about the murky water, he'd simply blame it on a bad filter and replace it, giving the tank a good cleaning while he was at it.

Best of all, it would show Little Mackey's buddies what happens when they give disapproving looks to their Brennan-God.

Two hours later, Little Mackey was still glaring at him.

Brennan was close to panic. Every moment he spent with the fish meant more of his control was slipping away.

When the longest shift he could remember finally ended, he raced all the way home, spurred to desperate energy by the memory of the other reptiles, birds, and small animals that populated the pet store.

All of them had stared at him accusingly, too.

~

Brennan spent some quality time with his good buddy *Jack Daniels* that night. He was determined to wash away all thoughts of the pet store jury. Between gulps, he cursed Billy Mackey's name and his Godforsaken fish.

Around midnight, during a rather intense rant, Brennan slurred his words and pronounced Mackey as "Mackerel." The irony dropped him to the floor in a fit of hysterical laughter.

But as his alcohol-induced gaiety slowly faded away, despair crept back in like an ocean fog, obscuring everything with its cold invasiveness. A distorted face peered through the mist, floating through Brennan's drunken haze.

The eyes were unmistakable.

Get out of my head!

But the mental specter of Billy Mackey sitting in that darkened basement, with those accusing eyes, remained.

Brennan heaved an old wicker chair at the wall out of frustration, losing his balance and collapsing onto the floor.

Why can't I put Mackey behind me? What is it about that kid?

Distorted images of the boy were projected onto the screen of Brennan's mind: a slideshow of bloodied knuckles; pants wetting, and cries of terror in the darkness.

Brennan's thoughts transported him back in time, to his harrowing experiences as a child in the basement of his house. To the terror of those countless, merciless beatings he'd received from his father in the yawning darkness. The gut wrenching feeling of betrayal—it all came crashing back.

He'd seen that look of betrayal on Mackey's face that day.

At that moment, for the first time since as far back as he could remember, Brennan felt tears welling up.

He threw back another swig of liquid forgetfulness and noticed a familiar black fish—wriggling inside his bottle of *Jack Daniels*. It dove straight down toward his throat.

He flung the bottle away in horror. It shattered against the far wall, spraying the room with alcohol and shards of glass. He spun around in a frenzy and looked for any signs of the little terror. He wanted to see it flopping on the carpet, gasping its final breath. But after a futile search, he finally collapsed onto the floor, woozy from the exertion.

It was a drunken hallucination, he thought. Or worse: a conscience that he didn't want.

On that final disturbing thought—he passed out cold.

~~~

Brennan was grateful for his brain-splitting hangover the next morning; it helped distract him from the fear of facing the pet store again. He gave the performance of a lifetime, acting as if nothing had changed when he strolled through the front door, maintaining the pretense that the animals remained his royal subjects.

As he moved through the narrow aisles of the store, he felt the eyes of the entire pet populace upon him. It unnerved him, but he refused to give them the satisfaction of a reaction. Instead, he focused on the day's steady stream of customers and did his best to avoid eye contact with the animals.

The reckoning was coming, of course. But he wanted it on *his* terms; and he knew that he would have the greatest advantage after store hours. Today was Sunday and the only day of the week the store closed early. He wouldn't have to deal with the usual idiots working the night shift.

Perfect.

When evening arrived, there was the usual feeding and cleaning to be done, as well as a dead pull that he'd already postponed from the day before. By the time he locked up the store, he'd finally mustered up the courage to face his bestial tribunal.

Time seemed to suspend as Brennan mopped the tile floor in the aquatics area, preparing for the face-off. He gradually—methodically—worked his way toward Little Mackey's tank. Now, more than ever, he felt its pervasive malice, like a pall of darkness over the room.

Brennan drew closer and closer with each wet swish of his mop, until he was finally standing next to the tank. He bent down to look at the hideous little thing; his face mere inches from the glass. The fish struck at him like an enraged snake, smacking against the glass with a resounding *thunk*. Brennan stumbled back, knocking over his bucket of dirty mop water.

The entire store rose up in a macabre cacophony: birds cawed, cats shrieked, puppies howled, and lizards hissed.

Brennan's mind began to scream, too. *Were they laughing at him? What the hell was happening here?*

As he took in the nightmarish spectacle, he realized that he'd crossed the point of no return. If he didn't make a stand now, he would no longer be seen as their king—but as the royal fool. He forced himself to meet the stare of the little black fish, fury buzzed in his ears like a swarm of enraged bees. His breath was forced and ragged as he rose to his feet.

The fish glared back.

Mocking him!

A mental dam inside Brennan's mind broke.

He smashed through the store like a river of rage, ignoring the screeches, barks and squawks that taunted him at every turn. He was searching for anything to kill the fish with, all pretense at finesse evaporated. It didn't matter what it was, as long it could tear, rend, smash-

Kill!

He yanked open cupboards and drawers, his thickset

body tensed with rage, face twisted and feral. He came across a serrated knife he'd used only the day before to chop up vegetables for the reptiles.

Now he'd use it to chop up Little Mackey.

Just like sushi, a crazed voice said in his mind.

The pet store had become sheer pandemonium; every animal seemed to shriek for blood from behind their cages. Barking, squawking, hissing, shrieking—Brennan's ears rang and his aching head whirled.

He raced toward the aquatics area. In his mind's eye, he could see the little black monstrosity impaled on his knife, wriggling in agonized death throes. He charged toward Little Mackey's tank.

The black fish glanced down at the wet, slippery floor with a knowing look.

Brennan saw it coming then, but he didn't have time to stop. He felt a moment of lost equilibrium and then he was lighter than air. His momentum carried him all the way across the room.

Upon impact, his face smashed straight through one of the aquariums. A thick shard of glass impaled his throat; turning the contents of the fish tank into a crimson waterfall.

Brennan hung there, flopping back and forth. Not unlike a fish out of water, gasping for air.

He'd missed Little Mackey's aquarium by half an arm's length.

The shimmering fish swam over from the neighboring tank to watch Brennan become the store's latest dead pull.

Brennan forced his gaze toward the hateful fish with his dying breath. What he saw there made him want to scream—though he physically could not.

Staring back at him was a grotesque little fish with Billy Mackey's eyes—filled with cold satisfaction.

Show and Tell

I'VE BEEN KEEPING something from you," Jacob said, staring at the floor. "And I don't want to lie to you anymore."

McDaniels adjusted the wire rim glasses at the far end of his nose. "It's an admirable thing to admit that."

For the first time since he'd entered the room, Jacob met McDaniels's eyes. "You know those pictures I drew? The ones that caused all the problems?"

McDaniels offered a comforting smile. "It's not that you caused any 'problems,' Jacob. Mrs. Finelli was simply concerned that you might have some feelings that you hadn't been able to express."

"I guess she was right," Jacob said, his eyes once more cast downward. "You can tell me whatever's on your mind. I'd like to help."

Jacob's eyes searched the tidy office. "Do you still have the pictures?"

"I do. Would you like to see them again?"

"No. I'd like you to see them again."

"Very well," McDaniels said. He stood up from behind his immaculate desk and reached for the student files in the metal cabinet directly behind him. He flipped through the sixth grade folders until he came upon one with the label: Campbell, Jacob.

Folder in hand, McDaniels sat back down in his swivel chair, which answered with a high-pitched squeak. He pulled out the series of colored pencil drawings that Mrs. Finelli had brought to his attention; Jacob had been secretly drawing them in class for several months.

McDaniels had seen a lot of disturbing drawings in his fifteen years as a school counselor, but these were particularly troubling. They were meticulously drawn and horribly realistic.

And the specificity of the illustrations raised unsettling questions: the dark basement, hospital bed, feeding pump, oxygen tanks, suction machines, and a whole array of medical equipment that the boy had drawn in explicit detail.

The subject of the twenty or so drawings, however, was what had prompted Mrs. Finelli to contact McDaniels in the first place. It was a ghastly, child-like thing that appeared to be bedridden and perpetually propped up at a forty-five degree angle by some kind of medical apparatus.

Its head was at least three times normal size, with bulging, green-colored veins covering the scalp, which seemed destined to explode from some urgent and terrible internal pressure. Its appendages were short, gnarled and incomplete.

Worst, by far, were the eyes. They looked like two translucent water balloons filled to bursting with blood, popping out beyond the normal boundaries of human eye sockets.

As McDaniels gazed upon the nightmarish drawings, it seemed as if the thing's crimson eyes were staring right through him. He found himself wanting to look away. While Jacob clearly had artistic talent, McDaniels hoped for the boy's sake that he would find different subject matter to explore in the future.

"Are you still having the nightmares?"

"Yes," Jacob stated, matter-of-factly. "Everything I've said about the nightmares is true. The part I lied about is that they are just nightmares." The boy's slender fingers fidgeted nervously with each other for long seconds before he spoke.

Then, in a quiet voice, "That thing in the drawings is . . . real."

McDaniels raised an eyebrow.

"It's . . . my brother."

McDaniels replied with what he felt was the appropriate level of gravity, "Really?"

"It's okay if you don't believe me."

"I didn't say I didn't believe you."

"Well, I wouldn't believe me if I were you. I mean . . . he looks like some kind of monster a kid would make up, right?" McDaniels offered his best noncommittal look, something he'd refined to perfection over the years.

Jacob continued, "His name's Quinn. He's a few years older than me, but I'm not sure by how much. I'm not supposed to ask questions about him."

McDaniels jotted something down in his notebook. "I see.

Why do you think that is?"

"It wouldn't look good."

"How so?

Jacob gave a humorless snort. "C'mon, Mr. McDaniels. You know my dad's position. He can't let the world know he hides a freak son in his basement."

McDaniels continued writing. "Can you explain what you mean by 'hides?'"

Jacob held himself as if he were sitting at a bus stop in the dead of winter. "We have this . . . basement. It's in the east wing of the house. I didn't know it was there until recently, 'cause I've never been allowed to go into the east wing. My parents have always kept it blocked off, except when we've had guests. And even then, we've never gone to that side of the house.

"I've grown up with a bunch of different gardeners, pool cleaners, housekeepers, and helpers around. It has always been off limits to them, too. But one day last November I was playing hide and go seek with a friend of mine out in the back, and I noticed one of the helpers— Lucinda—go through a back door in the east wing, a door that no one was supposed to use.

"I started watching her for a few days, and I saw that she went through that door about the same time every day. So, I snuck into the east wing early one morning and hid in a closet by the back entrance, and when she came into the house I followed her.

She was always talking and gossiping on her phone so she didn't notice me. I saw her go all the way to the end of the main hallway and into the very last room.

"I waited a couple of minutes, until I thought it was safe. Then I peeked inside the room and saw that she'd moved one of those . . . what do you call it . . . those big carpets from China?"

"An oriental rug?" McDaniels offered.

"Yeah, one of those. There was a big wooden door underneath it and a ramp that went all the way down to a basement. I don't think Lucinda worried about closing it, 'cause she didn't think anyone was around. I started to sneak down the ramp real quiet."

Jacob paused then, his thin face pinched with distaste. "I wish . . . I'd never gone down there."

McDaniels glanced at the thing in the drawings again.

He'd seen pictures of babies with massive heads that looked similar. He couldn't remember the proper medical term for it, but he knew it was sometimes referred to as "water on the brain." Jacob's interpretation, however, was more like something out of a horror film.

He watched the boy squirming in his chair for a few moments, and then said, "And what did you see?"

Jacob's eyes grew wider, as if the scene were unfolding before him. "I saw Lucinda changing an IV bag. I knew what it was, 'cause I'd seen them on TV. But I couldn't see who was lying in the hospital bed from where I was standing. I tried to get a better look, but I slipped and fell on the ramp.

Lucinda heard me and turned around . . . and I saw my brother for the first time. I started screaming. Lucinda tried to calm me down, but I couldn't stop screaming. I was still screaming after she'd carried me to the other side of the house and my parents came running.

"When my dad found out what I'd done, he wouldn't even look at me. He was so mad he punched a hole in the wall and sent me to my room. But my mom came to see me late that night, after Dad went to sleep. She'd been drinking a lot—I could always tell. She just fell on my bed and started crying and crying and crying. I'd never seen her like that before."

Jacob's eyes welled with tears, but he seemed to be doing his best to hold them back. "She told me everything."

McDaniels found his box of Kleenex and offered one. The boy shook his head and toughed it out. "I'm OK. It kinda feels good to talk about it—even though you probably don't believe me."

McDaniels cleared his throat. "I'm not here to judge the truth. I'm here to listen and help if I can."

The boy studied him, as if trying to discern whether or not he believed his words. McDaniels offered a vague smile and prepared to take more notes.

"Mom told me that what I'd seen down in the basement wasn't a monster. It was her first child. Quinn. They'd built him a special room. He even had his own private nurse—Lucinda. She said Quinn was born with a whole bunch of stuff wrong with him—things I can't even pronounce.

He couldn't see, talk, hear . . . anything. And his head is so big 'cause of his soft skull—and his brain. It's a lot bigger than normal.

"Mom said he came out that way because of a drug she took to help her get pregnant, 'cause she and dad couldn't have a baby on their own. It was an experimental drug that my dad's company made, but it caused all kinds of problems with babies."

Jacob's expression grew heavy with sorrow. "I asked her why she and Dad never told me before, and she said that they'd been waiting till I was old enough to understand. I was like, understand what? And that's when she told me that I was adopted . . ."

The boy's voice trailed off. Neither he nor McDaniels spoke for a full minute. The only sound in the room was the hollow clunk of the air conditioner as it came to life.

Finally, McDaniels broke the silence, "How did that make you feel, Jacob? Finding out that you were adopted?"

Jacob gave a quick shrug. "I don't know. Kinda mad. Kinda sad. Both at the same time, I guess. Know what I mean?"

"Of course," McDaniels said sympathetically. "That's understandable."

"I mean, I could see why they adopted me . . . after what happened to Quinn and all. They didn't want to take any chances, you know? What I couldn't understand was what she told me after that."

McDaniels took a deep breath as he flipped to the last blank page of his pad.

"Did you know that we only use about ten percent of our brains?" Jacob asked.

McDaniels nodded. "I've heard speculation to that effect . . . yes."

"Well, Mom said that Quinn can do things with his brain that we can't. But . . . he can't control it. And that's why they kept him drugged up and down in the basement. She said he did bad things when he was awake. I asked her how he could do bad things if he couldn't talk, hear, or move. And she couldn't answer me. All she could do was cry."

A tear dropped silently onto Jacob's cheek and a quiver crept into his voice. "She kept asking me to forgive her . . . telling me how much she loved me over and over."

Jacob wiped at his face. "The last thing she said before she left my room was: 'I'm sorry.'"

McDaniels handed the box of Kleenex to Jacob again, and this time the boy took a single tissue and wiped his eyes. "She died just a few hours later. Dad said that it was an accident, but I just know she took those pills on purpose."

McDaniels softened his voice, "I was very sorry to hear of your loss, Jacob. I understand how difficult that can be."

Jacob nodded, his face looking bloodless under the unflattering fluorescent lights. "I prayed that Quinn would get better. I'd always wanted a brother to play with. And every time I thought about him . . . stuck down in that cold basement alone, I would get so sad. Dad said that Quinn's brain didn't work like ours. He didn't know where he was, or what was going on. But I thought what if he was wrong?

"What if Quinn had known what was happening all those years but couldn't say or do anything about it? It was the worst thing I could think of.

"One night I found my dad drunk on the living room floor. It was always easy to get him to do things when he was drunk. He really wanted to sleep, but I kept bugging him about visiting Quinn and asking him for the combination to the lock on the basement door. He finally gave it to me just to get rid of me. But I didn't have the guts to go down there for a few more weeks.

"When Christmas came we didn't even put up a tree. That was something my mom was always in charge of. I searched all over the house Christmas morning, but I couldn't find my dad anywhere. I wanted to give Quinn a Christmas present so I finally went down to the basement by myself.

I saw my brother just laying down there in the dark, not moving at all, but staring at me with those awful eyes. I tried not to look at him too much, because he still scared me. But I'd brought him my favorite Batman comic as a present, and I started to read to him.

"And then, the weirdest thing happened . . . his breathing changed. It seemed calmer, and it made me feel good to think that might be because I was there. So I started visiting him a lot, and I always brought a stack of comics with me. My dad didn't seem to mind, as long as I didn't touch anything. And Quinn . . . I think he liked the visits.

But whenever Lucinda came down, I hated it 'cause she was always acting like I was in the way. But I was quiet and watched what she did, because I wanted to know how to take care of Quinn, too. I mean . . . he was my brother and all."

McDaniels reached into the organizer on his desk,

picked up a fresh pad of paper, flipped it open and started writing.

"You talk about Lucinda in the past tense. Is she no longer with you?"

Suddenly, Jacob smashed his fist down on the arm of his chair, giving McDaniels a hell of a start. "It's my fault it happened—but I could never have known it would happen!"

McDaniels regained his composure and spoke reassuringly,

"It's okay, Jacob. It's okay. What happened to Lucinda?"

Jacob gave a distraught sigh. "Remember . . . when I said they kept Quinn drugged? Well, I found out what it was. I looked it up on my computer. Doctors call it a 'morphine drip.' They use it on people when they're in lots of pain—and they use it to help people die faster."

McDaniels's mask of impassivity had begun to slip; lines of concern invaded the corners of his eyes.

Jacob raised his voice angrily, "It was like they were trying to kill him or something! So I went down into the basement and I poked a hole in the bag with a needle. I wanted to help Quinn wake up."

The boy's eyes darkened as he continued, "I went down the next day to check on him and the door was already open. There was this terrible smell coming out, like bleach and chemicals and stuff. As soon as I went down the stairs, I saw my dad. He'd moved Quinn and his bed to the far side of the basement and was cleaning up something off the floor with a mop. He was acting really weird, like he was sleepwalking or something.

There was blood everywhere, and this . . . twisted-up thing pushed into the corner. I couldn't tell what it was, at first. It kind of looked like a body, but it was turned inside out . . . like a coat when you can see the pockets . . . all these guts and organs and stuff on the outside.

"Then I saw Lucinda's bloody shoes lying in the corner and I knew. The horrible thing on the ground was all that was left of her. I got dizzy and my legs went wobbly—and that's the last thing I remembered before I woke up in my room.

My dad was just sitting there next to my bed, staring at me, bloodstains all over his shirt."

McDaniels was so intent on the boy's story that his pen slipped from his hands onto the desk. He quickly snatched it up and returned to his note taking.

Jacob spoke as if there were something unpalatable in his mouth, "He sat there and lied to my face; told me that Lucinda had a little accident with some of the medical equipment. Said he'd called an ambulance and she'd be just fine. I asked him about the bloody thing on the floor and he told me I'd hit my head—probably just imagined it.

I wanted to laugh in his face. I mean, how stupid did he think I was? But I pretended to believe him 'cause I didn't like the way he kept looking at me—I just wanted to get him out of my room.

"I couldn't sleep at all that night. I kept thinking about Quinn, and how my mom said he did bad things when he was awake. And now I knew what she meant. Somehow Quinn had done that horrible thing to Lucinda."

Light glinted off of the boy's cheeks, which were wet with tears. "And it's all my fault for waking him up."

McDaniels remained silent. He didn't want to risk Jacob shutting down again, as he had so many times in the past.

Jacob regarded his small hands as he spoke, "The next morning, I found out that Dad had fired the house staff: the housekeepers, gardeners, pool cleaners—everyone. He said it was just going to be him, Quinn, and me from now on, one big happy family. And when he said it, there was this smile on his face that didn't look right.

"Things only got worse after that. My dad moved Quinn's hospital bed into the family room, close to one of the windows—probably the first time he'd ever been near the sun. It was also the first time I'd seen Quinn fully awake.

He looked even scarier in the daylight. The veins in his head had gotten thicker. His eyes were redder, and they bulged even more. His face—it twitched a lot, like he was always in pain.

"And my dad . . . he became a completely different person. He'd never been interested in anything except his job before, but now his whole life was about my brother. He took personal leave from work so he could take care of Quinn. He cleaned him, fed him, and took care of whatever he needed.

"That's when it hit me. Quinn had to be controlling him—with his mind. That was why they'd kept Quinn drugged up all the time: to keep him from doing bad things with his mind! It was my brother that made dad clean up that mess with Lucinda.

That's why he was acting like he was sleepwalking when he did it. He also forced my dad to fire the house staff— and bring him out of the basement, too. I know my dad never would've done any of that stuff on his own— especially take leave from his job.

"It was right around then that my nightmares started, too. The ones I told you about—where Quinn's thoughts are in mine."

Jacob suddenly stood up. His eyes were scrunched shut, as if a sharp pain were lancing through his head.

"What is it?" McDaniels said with genuine concern.

The boy pounded his fist against his head. Once. Twice. Three times. "He's in my head right now. I can't get him out of my head!"

McDaniels tried calming words, but they felt hollow even as he said them. "It's okay, Jacob. Everything's going to be okay-"

The boy's eyes snapped open and he gave McDaniels a look that stopped him cold. "No, it's not. It's not gonna be okay at all."

McDaniels raised his hands. "I can see you're upset. And I'm here to listen. But I need you to relax and take a seat. Can you do that for me?"

Jacob met his gaze defiantly for a long and uncomfortable moment. Finally, he plopped back down in his chair, rubbing his temples; his face a taut mask of resistance.

"Maybe we should continue this later, Jacob."

"No!" Jacob snapped. "I still have to tell you the most important part—the whole reason I'm here."

McDaniels exhaled loudly. "Okay. I'm listening."

"Quinn . . . he tells me things. Not in words. It's more like . . . I can feel what he feels. And all he seems to feel is hate—especially for what my parents did to him. He wants to do terrible things to my dad—even worse than what he did to Lucinda. But I won't let him. I had to explain that killing him would be bad for both of us. We need a grownup for money, food, electricity and stuff.

But in some ways, it's as if my dad is already gone. Quinn's turned him into this thing—like a zombie that only looks like my dad. It's awful to see."

McDaniels's hand was cramping up from all the writing, but he didn't dare stop. He wanted to make sure he got everything down.

Jacob's fingers unconsciously probed the area around his eyes. "When Quinn is in my head, he can see and learn about the world through me; like when I'm watching TV or using my computer.

But his brain doesn't work the same—he learns way faster. He can scan a whole webpage in a few seconds. He wants me to keep clicking page after page . . . I can barely keep up with him.

"And then a few weeks ago he started having me bookmark all of these terrible news stories. The news people call them 'freak accidents.' Like a few weeks ago when all of those kindergarten kids on that school bus stopped breathing for no reason.

And then there was a gas explosion that destroyed a bunch of warehouses that my dad's company owns. Killed over a hundred employees. And everyone on the news is talking about these crazy fires that keep happening all over the city. I have over fifty bookmarks of things like that.

"I don't know how, but I think Quinn makes these things happen.

"But what scared me more than anything, were the two bookmarks from yesterday. The first one was a website about meltdowns at nuclear power plants and how they happen. And the second one was about the nuclear plant in our town."

Jacob paused for a moment and studied McDaniels's face. "I can tell that you don't believe me."

McDaniels reached under his glasses and rubbed his eyes before answering. "What's important here is that you believe it, Jacob. And I'm glad that you trusted me enough to tell me what's been troubling you."

Jacob reached for his backpack, which was sitting near his feet on the floor. It was faded black with a yellow

Batman logo emblazoned upon on it, and it appeared to be filled to the bursting point.

"You remember 'Show and Tell,' don't you, Mr. McDaniels?"

McDaniels nodded as he reached for the small bottle of water on his desk. He unscrewed the cap and began to drink.

His throat was so constricted and dry that it actually hurt.

Jacob said, "You're probably wondering why I would tell you all of this—stuff that could get my family in trouble." He unzipped his backpack and stepped closer to McDaniels's desk.

"It's because I knew you wouldn't believe me. And even if you did, it wouldn't matter . . . 'cause you're not leaving this room alive."

McDaniels choked on his water.

Jacob's face transformed then. His features took on a hateful, savage quality. "You told me everything I said in this room was confidential, Mr. McDaniels. But you lied. When you and Mrs. Finelli called my dad about those drawings, you broke your promise. I trusted you."

McDaniels wiped water from his chin with a trembling hand. "Listen . . . Jacob. It's true that our conversations are confidential. But teachers and counselors have the right to contact parents under certain circumstances."

Jacob moved awkwardly—as if he weren't in complete control of his body. "You thought you were talking to my dad, but you were wrong."

McDaniels started to respond, but he could only muster a weak gurgling sound.

Jacob reached into his backpack. "Mrs. Finelli didn't show up for school today because I visited her at her home last night—and I told her the same story I told you."

McDaniels stood up, struggling for his next breath, and then doubled over from a severe jolt of pain to his abdomen.

Jacob yanked Mrs. Finelli's severed head from his backpack. There were two gaping holes where her eyes had been, and her blood-streaked face was stretched into a hideous, eternal scream. McDaniels dropped to the floor in agony as his internal organs began to shift and twist, like a pit of snakes had been unleashed inside his body.

The boy McDaniels knew as Jacob Campbell stood over him, his face twitching, as if he was in pain. At that moment, the school counselor realized that everything the boy had said was true.

The last thing McDaniels saw, as his torso split open and his insides began to push their way out, was the boy staring down at him with familiar, bulging red eyes.

THE INFECTED

MY FATHER'S BODY, blood and other excretions had been removed—but his bedroom still reeked. Maybe the smell was real; maybe it was imagined. But I think it takes a lot more than industrial chemicals to scrub away a death like that.

That type of thing tends to linger.

The apartment manager gave me thirty days to clear out my dad's stuff. I waited until the thirtieth day. If there hadn't been a tight deadline, I might not have done it at all. It's not the kind of thing you look forward to. It would be so much nicer to remember things the way they were, instead of how they are.

I stood in the center of Dad's bedroom—where he'd taken his old 12-gauge shotgun, pressed the barrel under his thick chin, and turned his head into something not unlike a giant burst tomato. That was my first thought when I'd had to identify his body; an image I would spend the rest of my life trying to flush from my mind.

The cleanup crew had ripped up most of the carpet, which had been showered with bits and pieces of the man I'd once believed was invulnerable. Unstoppable. Invincible.

As I scanned what was left of the furnishings in his room, I could no longer deny how far he'd fallen. He'd sold off anything of value at the pawnshop down on Western

Ave., and all that was left looked like the unwanted dregs of a long forgotten garage sale.

The clean up experts had removed anything defiled by human matter. All that remained were a couple of cardboard boxes filled with dog-eared science fiction paperbacks, a stack of twenty year-old TV guides that Dad had saved for the crossword puzzles, and a handful of tattered pictures of our family of three—back when Mom was still alive.

Guardedly, I peeked inside the closet—and gagged. The clothes hanging there were permeated with fifteen years of cigarette smoke. I recognized some of the shirts immediately. Without Mom around to buy him new clothes, Dad had been rotating the same ten to fifteen shirts for years.

I was about to start cleaning out the closet when I noticed something shoved against the far wall. As my brain registered what it was, I felt fingers of dread reaching up to constrict my throat.

It was Dad's old army footlocker.

The Army green, metal box looked exactly the same as it had twenty-five years earlier when I'd first discovered it. It had been hidden in our garage, back when we lived in a two-story house in Encino. The footlocker was dented, scratched, and had two rusted bullet holes that ventilated the front—presumably from Dad's stint in Vietnam.

I'd been eight years old at the time and had tried to jimmy the padlock with a paper clip, like I'd seen them do on old TV shows. I'd sat on the cold, cement floor of the garage for over half an hour, failing miserably at my new career as a lock picker.

Suddenly, a large specter stepped out of the shadows and I screamed.

It was my father. He saw what I was attempting and proceeded to give me the beating of my life.

I'd understood that what I'd done was wrong, of course. But the severity of the punishment hardly matched the crime. What had disturbed me most was the look in his eyes; *he* seemed more scared than I was, scared of what I'd find inside.

I never dared to go through his things again.

Now, as I stood in my father's closet, surrounded by the pervasive stench and yellow-stained walls, I felt like that little boy again, about to unforgivably invade my father's privacy. I half-expected his ghost to creep up from behind me and shout: *'You want another beatin', boy?'*

I backed out of the closet.

I just couldn't face the prospect of opening the footlocker; not yet, at any rate.

Later that day I tried to donate Dad's stuff to Goodwill. Most of it was tragically outdated, dirty or just plain useless. The disinterested woman at the counter would only accept his old television set and the stack of books. I guess even the needy have their standards. I ended up throwing the rest of it away, except for the box of pictures, and of course, the footlocker.

It took several glasses of wine and a home cooked meal from my wife, Megan, but my mood lightened considerably by that evening. She did her best to distract me with future plans for our first child, Emma, who was due in four months. I was nervous as hell about being a parent, but Megan's enthusiasm helped balance it out.

"I found the greatest little outfit for Emma at the mall yesterday," she said, while nibbling at the remainder of her roasted potatoes. "Embroidered on the chest it says: 'Do infants enjoy infancy as much as adults enjoy adultery?'" Her grin caused dimples to indent her lovely pale cheeks.

I laughed despite myself. "That's horrible. Your mom will hate it."

"*I know*," Megan said with mock maliciousness.

I smiled back, desperate to hold onto the light mood. We gabbed about more baby nonsense for a while, but it wasn't long before the reality of our financial situation seeped in like a bottle of spilled ink.

The money I'd earned on my last novel was nearly gone, and for the past few months I'd been faced with the reality of getting a second job. Now, with my dad's funeral expenses added to the mix, we'd jumped head first into the red.

I'd started two mystery novels and a poorly conceived science fiction opus since my last published work, but hadn't gotten past the third chapter on any of them. My muse had left me like a jilted wife after a long court battle, taking both my money and self-respect. I'd had three years of unrelenting writer's block, and even my once enthusiastic literary agent had written me off.

I'd bitten the bullet and signed up with several employment agencies over the past month, but the recession wasn't improving and even the lowliest of temp jobs had become scarce.

As I poured myself another glass of wine, I remembered something: a classified ad I'd cut from one of those employment newspapers you see in the free bins. It had sat crumpled on my desk for weeks. The headline read:

WRITERS! ACTORS! DIRECTORS!
TIRED OF WAITING TABLES?
GUARANTEED WORK!

Guaranteed work.

I didn't believe in such things, but I admit the ad piqued my curiosity; I'd seen it floating around town for years, and was understandably skeptical. At the same time, desperate times called for desperate measures, and I figured if the company were a complete sham, I'd discern it quickly enough.

I told Megan about it and she supported the decision. We both knew that her maternity leave was going to kill us financially. She was a former starving actress turned full-time customer service representative, and didn't make a lot of money. But it was the only steady income we had.

With limited options and abject poverty looming on the horizon, I decided to call the number in the ad the next day.

As we lay together in bed that night, Megan asked me about the footlocker that I'd pushed to the back of our bedroom closet.

I pretended not to hear her, rolled over and shut my eyes.

~~~

The name of the company in the ad—*The Tempting Agency*—was of course, a silly play on the word "temp." But the woman I spoke with was all business. Before I knew it, she'd scheduled me for a computer test and interview. She told me that if I qualified for their services I'd be guaranteed a booking within twenty-four hours.

Twenty-four hours.

Unfortunately, there wasn't an opening for an interview until the following Monday, so I sat around the apartment for most of the week, doing nothing but avoiding my manuscripts, avoiding the footlocker, and waiting for Megan to come home to rescue me from my thoughts.
~~~

After four days of flipping channels and suffering through endless commercials for law firms and trade schools, it became clear that the only people who watched daytime TV were the unemployed, injured or disabled. And I didn't plan on being any of the three.

I decided to go for a walk to clear my head and pray to the Gods of Literature for the return of my muse. I didn't have to go that far, though; my muse was waiting for me in the next room. I noticed it as I was getting dressed for my walk: the footlocker on the floor of my closet. It stared at me mutely, like a small metal creature with two rusted bullet holes for eyes.

What the hell was I so scared of? The more I thought about it, the more I realized how childish I had been, building up the malevolence of the footlocker to the point of absurdity. I laughed then, imagining myself opening it after all these years, only to find a well-worn stack of girly magazines.

I lugged the footlocker into the living room; poured myself a glass of wine, downed it in one shot, and poured another. I jangled my dad's set of keys in my hand absently; they had been given to me by a police officer the same night I identified the body. Sure enough, in between his house key, his mail key and two unknowns, was an archaic one that looked to be Army-issue.

I steeled myself as I inserted it into the war-torn lock and turned, holding my breath as it popped open. I thought of Pandora as I lifted the metal lid.

Glancing at the innards of the box, I gave a massive sigh of relief. There were no rusted knives stained with blood, or grinning skulls from the Vietnamese soldiers my dad had killed in 'Nam (as my eight year-old mind had once imagined).

One at a time, I removed the contents.

The first item was a plastic-wrapped hardcover book called *Chaos Signal*, my father's only published book, and nearly impossible to find anywhere—God knows I'd tried. It was in perfect condition and I was thrilled to have such a pristine copy. I'd found a decent used copy online a few years back, but this one looked like it had never been cracked open.

Underneath that was a crumpled stack of typewritten short stories in various stages of completion—all were unpublished; next was a black and white photo of my dad and grandfather standing on some unknown lakeshore. My father looked to be about eight or nine years old, and was struggling to hold up a catfish about half his size. He was grinning so wide that his mouth threatened to swallow his ears. To see him that happy brought tears to my eyes.

My grandfather—who had died of a heart attack when I was seven years old—also looked quite pleased in the photo. It may have been the *only* time I'd seen Grandpa crack a smile. To see them both together and happy in the same photo was simply too much. All of the pain I'd bottled up since my dad's suicide came pouring out of me.

I took me quite some time to regain my composure, but eventually, my thoughts returned to the footlocker. I pulled out a fourth item: a folder made of faded brown leather and stuffed with 8 x 11 paper. I was immediately struck by the unmistakable smell of musty old paper. I opened to the first page and realized that I was looking at an unpublished manuscript written in longhand.

The title page read:

The Infected
By Robert Carter

I felt the hairs on my neck stand on end. It was an unpublished novel written by my father! His book *Chaos Signal* was a wonderfully imaginative science fiction novel, and had inspired me greatly in my youth. I had no idea that he'd written another book.

The opening paragraph read:

It is beyond the bounds of my pen to describe what I have seen deep within the walls of the Grayston Building, so that you might imagine it in your mind as I see it in my nightmares each night. For within the shadowy recesses of the Grayston Building, a dark monolith that stands in the heart of the Chicago business district, there are things that no modern man can conceive.

The protagonist of the novel, Jonathan Conner, is a well-meaning, if somewhat naïve young man who dreams of one day becoming an architect. The dream, however, begins to float adrift when his father becomes gravely ill and can no longer subsidize Jonathan's education. Disheartened, the young man leaves college and moves back home to help take care of his family. With limited job experience, he takes the best job he can find: mailroom runner at a public accounting firm called Grayston & Co. The pay is low, but it helps keep food on the table for his father, mother and two younger siblings.

Before long, Jonathan discovers something rather disturbing at Grayston. While delivering mail to the various floors of the building, he notices that most of the employees shuffle through the halls like well-dressed zombies, with soulless eyes that stare right past him.

With each passing day, he feels more like an outsider. His coworkers seem to be devoid of creative thinking, presence, awareness, intellectual curiosity, or humor. It's as if he's the only person at Grayston with any personal vitality.

Jonathan becomes fearful of his fellow employees, fearful of the contagion that seems to have spread throughout the building. He tells himself that zombies only exist in horror stories and films, but the more he observes his coworkers, the less alive they appear to be.

One evening at a burger joint after work, Jonathan runs into Brian Cort: a former college buddy. After the usual pleasantries, the inevitable subject of work comes up. When Jonathan mentions his job at Grayston, Brian laughs, though in a rather forced way. "I survived a summer internship there," he says, "and barely escaped with my life. I actually lost points in my performance appraisal for being 'too enthusiastic'."

Jonathan tries to laugh, too, but it feels just as manufactured as Brian's.

Brian takes a long look into Jonathan's eyes—as if searching for something. He says, gravely, "Something isn't right about that place. You know that, right?"

Jonathan tries to grin but it comes off more like a grimace, "Sure, we used to joke about corporate bottom line mentality back in sociology class."

"No, I'm talking about dehumanization like we never imagined back in school. That company won't be satisfied until they've sucked your soul dry. Don't get too comfortable there," he warns Jonathan. "I'd hate to see you turning into one of *them*."

I stopped reading my father's novel for a moment and reflected. The themes resonated and I particularly liked my father's use of the concept of infection as a metaphor for the disillusioned, the hopeless and the countless masses living in quiet desperation.

I continued reading until early evening when I was abruptly taken out of the story by a handwritten note alongside the margins of the manuscript.

It read:

Life imitating art . . . or the reverse? The longer I stay at Hudson and Weiss, the more I find myself struggling to separate the two. I'm beginning to think that the people I work with may actually be infected. Writing this novel may be the only thing keeping me alive . . .

I had the startling realization that I wasn't reading my father's handwriting after all—it was my grandfather's. I didn't know much about him; other than that he shared my father's name and, to my knowledge, had never smiled; except, apparently, in that one photo. When I saw the name *Hudson and Weiss*—purveyor of life insurance and maudlin TV commercials—it clicked. My grandfather had worked there most of his life, until he'd died of a heart attack while sitting at his desk at work.

No one had noticed he had died for two full days.

The note that my grandfather had written to himself along the margin was odd to say the least, but I didn't realize its full impact until later.

I sat there for a while, absorbing the fact that Robert Carter Sr. had been a writer, too. Apparently, the apples didn't fall far from the trees in the Carter family. It unnerved me—like I'd just discovered some dark family secret. Never in my life had I heard anyone speak about my grandfather's writings. I found that terribly disconcerting, considering the fact that my father was a published novelist and so was I.

The superlative manuscript in my hands made it clear that my grandfather had been writing for quite some time. You don't develop a skill like that overnight. But where was the rest of his work? I wondered if it had returned to dust along with its creator.

It seemed tragic that his book had never seen the light of day. My first instinct was to try to get it published posthumously. That is, if the rest of the story held up. It suddenly dawned on me that his manuscript might not be finished.

I began flipping through the pages.

At about the halfway point, the handwritten pages stopped, and the manuscript continued with typewritten ones. Folded up in the center were a handful of pages filled with random story notes. I scanned them and immediately recognized my father's stationery. I couldn't believe it; I was looking at story notes on my grandfather's manuscript from my own father.

The notes contained interesting new directions for the plot and various thoughts about the manuscript. Many of the ideas had been scratched out; and as I sifted through them I began to piece together a story of my own. From what I could sort out, my grandfather had given up on the manuscript at some point, though the reasons weren't clear. My father's desire had been to complete the book as co-author, and get it published as a tribute to his father.

Suddenly, the manuscript took on a beautiful new meaning: it was a written testament to the love Robert Carter Junior had for Robert Carter Senior.

I was holding a priceless artifact.

I felt a renewed admiration for my father at that moment, and a connection to my grandfather that I'd never felt before.

Megan came home about then and I rushed into the living-room to tell her all about the treasure I'd found.

~~~

"Your test scores are excellent," the man named Mills said. "Typing speed is above par, too."

I smiled from the other side of Mill's immense black desk, knowing I'd aced the software and typing tests. Now
~~~

it was just a matter of winning him over with my personality—never an easy task for me, not being much of a people person. Perhaps that's why I was a writer.

I gave Mills the once over as he finished scanning my test results. He was literally the most nondescript person I'd ever met; if he ever decided to rob banks, there would be no need for a mask.

He perused my professional resume, glanced over to size me up, and firmly smoothed the paper out on the surface of his immaculate desk.

"I see you're a writer. Film . . . or TV?"

I winced a little. In Los Angeles, writers are assumed to be solely interested in film or television. Mention you're a novelist at an L.A. cocktail party, and people stare at you like you have a second penis—sticking out of your forehead.

"Neither." I maintained a pleasant tone. "I'm a novelist."

Mills smiled thinly. "Oh. Well, some of our *finest* employees are in the arts. We recruit a lot of . . . your type."

I wasn't sure if he was intentionally trying to insult me, but I gave him the benefit of the doubt.

The interview crawled along like a police interrogation. Beneath Mills' plastered-on grin, it became obvious that he had a general disdain for creative types. I suspected that he was a frustrated artist himself; the city was teeming with them.

He droned on about confidentiality agreements, time sheets, holiday overtime and a laundry list of company policies. I tried to remain focused, but the lifelessness in his voice nearly put me to sleep.

Finally, he said: "Congratulations. You're part of the family now."

I refocused my attention on the man with the lacklustre face. And then I noticed it. Something so subtle I hadn't perceived it before.

It was his eyes.

They looked . . . dead.

Mills called me a few hours later at home and I spoke with him through a fog of relief and anxiety. I had a fair amount of experience as a temp employee, and knew it was a daily crapshoot. One day you would land a pleasant gig in a luxurious office, and the next you'd find yourself slaving away in a rat's nest under the rule of the Anti-Christ.

"Good news," Mills said. "You're scheduled for a five-day assignment at Capital-Co., starting tomorrow; one of our biggest clients; a real estate capital investment firm." He informed me that Capital-Co. had topped *America's Most Admired Companies* list in *Fortune* magazine and that their hourly rate was higher than industry standard. They even supplied free bagels on Mondays and Fridays.

I shared the good news with Megan, and she was relieved, to say the least. She showed her appreciation in bed that night. Normally, I slept like a baby afterward, but all I could think about was finishing the manuscript I'd started.

Despite having to get up early the next day for my temp assignment, I stayed up late reading *The Infected*. I was desperate to know what happened to Jonathan, particularly as I neared the end of the handwritten section of the manuscript, the point at which my grandfather had stopped writing—and my father had taken over.

Jonathan toils away for another year at Grayston, working his way up from the mailroom into an entry-level job in the accounts department. With his father's accumulating medical bills, it becomes clear that his dreams of returning to college are moving farther and farther away.

His father has become a withered shell of a man, loose, bloodless folds of skin draped over his brittle frame. One night, not long before he dies, he confides in Jonathan. In between rasping breaths, he tells him that Bernice—Jonathan's mother—is a lying whore and has been cheating on him.

Jonathan is appalled at the accusation. "Don't be ridiculous," he exclaims. "When would she have time? She's your caretaker all day long."

His father gives a wretched laugh, raw with physical and emotional pain. "My caretaker? That whore disappears for hours with no explanation, smelling of cheap men's cologne whenever she comes back."

Jonathan refuses to listen, unable to believe his mother capable of such a thing.

His father dies a week later.

When Jonathan feels that the appropriate amount of grieving has passed, he asks his mother when she plans to go back to the factory work she did before his father took ill. He's eager to re-enter college as a full-time architectural student, but knows that it will be impossible if he's also the family's single source of income.

His mother tells him that she's too depressed to work and begs for more time to adjust to life without his father.

Jonathan accepts this and bides his time in the hope that he can get his architectural degree through night school, even though it will take him at least twice as long to do it.

However, when one of Jonathan's friends spots his mother out on the town a few weeks later, being publicly affectionate with another man, he realizes that she's already "adjusted" just fine. He confronts her about it the next day. She flatly denies it.

And as he stares into his mother's eyes, he realizes that she is completely indifferent to his hopes and dreams. For the first time, he notices the deadness of her eyes; and to his growing horror, realizes that the infected can be anyone—even those you love most.

My grandfather's handwritten prose ended there.

I sat there immobile, processing the last chapter for quite some time. And like a jigsaw puzzle, pieces of my family's past began to drop into place. I remembered how my father spoke of my grandmother with such distaste. How she'd run off in the middle of the night when he was ten years old; left town to be with a traveling salesman who made more money than my grandfather ever could.

She never contacted them again.

My grandfather's life was laid bare before me in the manuscript, thinly disguised as a piece of fiction. I suddenly recalled my own mother telling me that John Carter Sr.'s lack of education had kept him stuck in a low-level supervisory position his entire career.

I knew then that my grandfather had died of shattered dreams and a broken heart; he hadn't completed the manuscript for *The Infected*, because he had become one of them.

I flipped back to the foreboding words that he'd written alongside the margin of the manuscript earlier, and a shiver seized me as I read it again.

Life imitating art . . . or the reverse? The longer I stay at Hudson and Weiss, the more I find myself struggling to separate the two. I'm beginning to think that the people I work with may be infected, and writing this novel is the only thing keeping me alive . . .

I slept terribly all night. In my dreams, my grandfather's pale, gnarled hands grasped at me through a writhing tapestry of darkness, and countless dead eyes peered out at me.

~

Sleep-deprived and groggy, I stepped into the lobby of the Capital-Co. building the next morning in my best work clothes. As I scanned the lobby, the austere, fluorescent lighting seemed to drain everything rather than illuminate it and the drab office furnishings and generic décor blended into a functional, but dreary landscape.

I stepped up to an imposing reception desk and tried to catch the attention of the middle-aged woman answering the phones. Her skin looked nearly as grey as the corporate logo on the wall.

She spoke into her earpiece with a hollow voice, "Thank you for calling Capital-Co., how may I direct your call?" She repeated this over and over with the same cadence. Finally, after a momentary lapse in calls, she glanced at me.

"Yes?"

I gave my best *it's my first day, so I'm trying to make a good impression* smile and said, "I'm from the Tempting Agency. I was told to report to a . . . Denny Augustine?"

The phone lit up again, attracting the gray woman's attention. "File room," she said on automatic. "Take the elevator to the basement . . . follow it to the end."

She returned to the phone calls and her broken-record greetings. The dead sound of her voice haunted me all the way to the basement.

Exiting the elevator, I felt as if I'd just stepped into the bowels of the earth. The automatic door closed behind me with a *ting* and the silence that followed pressed in from all sides.

THE INFECTED

I wound my way through the innards of the building until I reached a cavernous room. I was startled by an imp of a man staring at me, standing directly in the center of the room with his hands clasped behind his back.

I wondered how long he'd been standing there.

"Hello . . . " the imp said. "Welcome to the file room."

Denny Augustine was a deadly serious little man. He'd spent the last fourteen years working deep in the innards of Capital Co.; and he smelled as musty as the mountains of files that surrounded us.

I was fatigued, but did my best to focus on his detailed explanation of the filing system. A dizzying swarm of words buzzed inside my head as the imp lectured me on the proper filing of tax compliance forms, K-1s, P&Ls, Audits, Investor Reports and an endless array of real estate financials.

I stifled a scream of delight when my lunchtime reprieve arrived like a governor's pardon at an execution.

During lunch I sat in a corner of the kitchen on the 18th floor (which had the best view of the city) and continued reading *The Infected*. I did my best to ignore the odd looks I illicited from everyone who passed by. Apparently, the act of sitting down and enjoying a lunch break was an alien concept for Capital Co. employees.

As I continued to read the manuscript, the first thing I noticed was that my father had adopted my grandfather's voice quite well.

It was mere days after my confrontation with Mother that I came to understand the depths of her callousness. When I arrived home that Friday evening, I discovered a handwritten note from her on the refrigerator. With a scant fifty-nine words, she forever changed the course of my life and how I would view the world.

Jonathan,

I have found someone to take care of me, and have sold both the house and the family car, as I have no need for either. You are a legal adult now, thus I am placing your siblings in your care. I trust you'll look after them in my absence, as I can no longer administer their needs.
Mother

I stopped reading for a moment and stared out the window. My father had taken the tragedy of his mother leaving him and integrated it into the novel. It made perfect sense—an obvious continuation of the manuscript.

My lunch hour seemed to fly by in seconds, and I soon found myself back in the dungeon disguised as a file room.

I spent the next few hours trying to get to know Denny Augustine, but he was as impenetrable as the seemingly countless files that filled the room. I noticed a travel poster for the Greek islands half-hidden behind some file folders on his desk. It caught my eye, because it was the only thing in the entire room with a modicum of color.

"I love the Greek Islands," I said, gesturing toward the image of Greece.

Denny looked at me, then the poster. It offered a breathtaking view of mountainous islands that seemed to climb straight out of the Aegean Sea. Denny stared at it with puzzlement, as if seeing it for the first time.

"Forgot that was there . . ." he said trailing off as he gently pulled the thumbtacks from the poster. And then an afterthought, " . . . a lifetime ago."

He folded it up carefully, and for a moment I thought he was planning to take it home. But then he shoved it into a recycling bin.

We spent the rest of the afternoon filing in silence.

When I returned home that night, I lied to Megan and told her that the temp job was great and quickly changed the subject. No good would come from complaining about it. After all, I would only be there for a week.

After dinner I cleaned the dishes, gave Megan a peck on the cheek, and hurried to my desk in the makeshift office in the guest bedroom (the bedroom I'd soon be giving up to our newborn). I was anxious to continue reading.

The next few chapters of *The Infected* took a darker, more fantastical direction. This wasn't a great surprise, as my father's work leaned toward dystopian science fiction.

In the novel, Jonathan is forced into the unlikely role of parent to his younger siblings: 11 year-old Stephanie and 14 year-old Paul. Between the pressure of taking care of his grieving brother and sister and working for a company that eats away at his soul, alcohol seems to be the only effective balm.

One night while working late, he hears an eerie shuffling noise echoing somewhere within the lonely halls of Grayston. He gets up from his desk to investigate, and staggers; intoxicated from his regular nipping at the whiskey he keeps hidden in the bottom drawer of his desk.

A movement catches his eye—a dark figure shuffles past. Startled, Jonathan almost falls again, unsteady on his feet.

"Evening," Jonathan calls out, but there is no response.

He follows the lumbering figure down the hall: a large man in a dark suit moving toward a set of double doors that lead to the finance department.

Intrigued, Jonathan continues after him, but his wobbly legs cause him to stumble. The man hears this and turns, just as Jonathan hides behind a pillar, his back pressed against the wall.

After what feels like a lifetime of waiting, he hears the double doors being unlocked. Cautiously, he peeks out with one eye. The broad shouldered man shambles inside a large and brightly illuminated room; beyond the door are rows upon rows of men and women, hunched over their desks like the shanghaied crew of an ocean-going vessel. Several of them move in unison, as if controlled by some sort of corporate *hive-mind.*

A handful of dark-suited men pace between the rows, like slave ship captains lording over their shackled crews.

As the door slowly begins to close, one of the nameless employees glances up from his work: a featureless man with vague holes where his eyes, nose and mouth should be.

Glancing around the section of the room that he can see, Jonathan realizes that everyone inside looks like an unfinished mannequin.

He has to stifle a scream as the door closes with a resounding *click.* He begins to run. And he doesn't stop running until he's safely in his car and screeching out of the parking lot.

At home, Jonathan stares into the bathroom mirror, scared sober. He tells himself that his mind is playing tricks on him. It isn't the first time he's seen something dark and twisted at the bottom of a whiskey bottle.

He tells himself that the office is always hectic near the end of the fiscal quarter, and that the faceless drones he saw were really just a bunch of accounting employees working late—garden variety bean counters, burning the midnight oil to get their yearly numbers in order.

But another voice in his head tells him something different. Jonathan suddenly recalls the words of his college buddy, Brian Cort, who said: *I'm talking about dehumanization like we never imagined back in school. That company won't be satisfied until they've sucked your soul dry."*

He shudders, realizing that his friend was being neither ironic nor metaphorical.

Jonathan gazes at his reflection, studies it with growing apprehension—and tells himself that the bland face staring back is just his imagination . . .

The next page of the manuscript was blank.

That was it—end of story. Just one more thing to add to my dad's long of list of unfinished business.

I went back through his detailed story notes. It was obvious he had intended to complete his father's novel. But nothing explained why he had stopped writing. Writer's block? Life's distractions? Or was it something more sinister?

I suddenly recalled the look on his face the day he'd caught me trying to open the footlocker; the fear in his eyes. I'd never been able to wrap my head around that.

Maybe I'd misinterpreted it. After all, I'd only been eight years old at the time. This was before my dad's only novel had been published, so perhaps he'd been ashamed of the large stack of unfinished work inside, a footlocker brimming with failure. That certainly fit his profile. Dad always seemed embarrassed that he wasn't more prolific, his responses always awkward when anyone asked him if he was going to write another book.

He had tried, of course. Tried and failed many times. But like his father before him, Robert Carter Jr. had finally resigned himself to a life of quiet desperation.

Determination gripped me. I wanted to honor the ghosts of my father and grandfather by finishing the manuscript. And yet, this wasn't a completely selfless act. It was a salable story, the kind of novel that could put me back on the map. And it already had a built-in marketing hook: a novel co-written by three generations of writers.

I flipped back to my grandfather's prophetic handwritten message, scrawled in the margin. He seemed to believe that writing the manuscript would somehow keep him from becoming infected. And deep down, I suppose I believed that finishing the manuscript would save me, too.

A boyhood memory appeared like an unwanted guest. It was the day my mother and I showed up unannounced at my father's workplace—as a surprise for his birthday. The dreary lighting and grey walls had struck me, and I was reminded of prison scenes I'd seen on TV. My dad sat slumped over a stack of paperwork, and there seemed to be a terrible sadness about him. It had made me want to cry, just seeing him like that.

When he spotted me walking toward him, his face lit up with all the love there was in the world. He jumped up and hugged me for so long that I finally got embarrassed and pulled away.

I still regret that.

After our visit, he hinted several times that we could visit him anytime. But I didn't want to go back to that awful place, couldn't bear the thought seeing him like that again.

Thirty years later, after he'd spent the better part of his life reviewing and processing an endless stream of internal forms and reports for a shipping company, he was downsized just six months short of retirement.

He took his own life not long after.

Angered, I slammed the leather-bound manuscript on my desk and went to bed, curling up next to Megan and placing my hand gently across her swollen belly. That night I had wretched dreams, inexorably drawn toward that veil of shadows where thousands of vacant eyes stared like glass marbles out at me. Leathery hands grabbed my arms; it was my grandfather again, trying to drag me down into his darkness.

The Infected

As I struggled to break free, something bit into my leg—ripping my flesh open.

I looked down to see a blood spattered face gazing up at me. A man with dead eyes.

My father.

I woke up screaming.

Despite the recurrent nightmares that plagued my nights, the days that followed seemed to soar past. My muse had returned like an insatiable lover; I hadn't written with such passion in years. If fact, I became so fixated with writing *The Infected* that when my temp assignment was extended, I didn't give it a second thought. Literally. Filing had become so rote by that point that I could spend most of the day plotting the book in my mind, and then get it down on paper at night.

Within a few weeks, Denny Augustine offered to extend my position in the file room indefinitely, and I agreed to stay for the time being. Megan was about to take maternity leave and I knew we'd need my steady paycheck while I finished the manuscript.

My wife would give birth to our baby daughter, and I would give birth to my first book in nearly four years.

The story dreamt up by my grandfather, and later advanced by my father, had become a self-fulfilling prophecy for both of them. I had no intention of following in their footsteps. I resolved to take the story in a new direction.

It was time for Jonathan, the hero of *The Infected*, to dig his way back from hell.

Finding the writing voice of my predecessors was a challenge, but after a few false starts, I managed it. However, what proved the most difficult was creating a plausible ending that honored what had come before, yet still satisfied my desire for a more hopeful conclusion. I'd written about spies, soldiers and wayward adventurers, but Jonathan's adversary wasn't some larger than life villain he could simply outsmart or beat up. Jonathan was just an ordinary man, fighting something far more insidious; an internal antagonist . . . an infection that killed hope and destroyed dreams.

The feeling was all too familiar, something I'd experienced after writing and producing a dismally received stage play about teenage runaways early in my career. Megan was still an actress back then and I had met her for the first time during auditions. She had received good notices for her performance, even if my play hadn't, and I'd nearly lost my shirt putting up the show.

I fell into a deep depression, convinced that I would spend the rest of my life in limbo as a temp employee. Megan was equally weary of being broke all the time, and we moved in together to split the rent. She took a much needed break from acting and I helped support her until she found a part-time job in customer service at a telecommunications company.

Megan encouraged me to continue writing while I worked as a temp all over town. When she read a rough draft of my first novel *American Underworld,* a revisionist look at the Al Capone era, she hounded me to finish it. When I did, she hounded me again until I submitted it to publishers.

We eventually fell in love, and Megan's faith is what carried me through those dark times. And the book that resulted is what launched my writing career—such as it is.

I knew that was what the protagonist of *The Infected* needed, too: someone to believe in him.

Picking up where my father had left off, Jonathan is desperate to escape from Grayston, terrified that he'll become another faceless drone. However, as the sole provider for his younger brother and sister, he knows he's trapped until he can line up another job. Times are tough, and with Jonathan's limited experience, options are few.

Deep in despair, everything changes for him the day he meets Sarah, a recently hired receptionist on the 3rd floor. She is the antithesis of the dispirited figures that haunt the halls of Grayston, and her radiance attracts him like a moth ticking at a light bulb.

Friendly flirtations blossom into a spring romance, and for the first time since he can remember, Jonathan doesn't feel alone. He and Sarah commiserate about the pall of enervated misery that hangs over Grayston. She finds his reference to "well-dressed zombies" both amusing and grimly true. Like Jonathan, she too dreams of a better life, and when they're together they spend much of their time talking passionately about their goals and aspirations.

Jonathan starts to feel hopeful again, and is able to stop drinking to get through the work day. Even the memory of the faceless drones he'd seen trapped behind the double doors begins to fade, and he convinces himself that it was merely a drunken hallucination.

And yet, the deadened eyes of the infected always seem to be upon him, and it isn't long before coworkers take notice of his budding romance with Sarah. They whisper to each other conspiratorially in the halls whenever he approaches and they stare at him and Sarah accusingly whenever they're together.

Jonathan becomes more motivated than ever to create

an exit strategy, and he plans to propose to Sarah the moment he's found a better job.

But he soon learns that the infected have no intention of letting him leave. They haunt him not only in his dreams, but also in his waking thoughts. Fear begins to eat away at his confidence and will, and he discovers that his greatest battle will be waged inside himself, against the first stage of infection, which has already started to spread . . .

I stopped work on the novel temporarily when Emma, our baby daughter, surprised us by showing up to the party two weeks early. By the grace of God, she got her mother's looks, and was more beautiful than I could have hoped for.

Megan and I had spent an inordinate amount of time researching what to expect during our first year of parenthood—for all the good it did us. The onslaught of sleepless nights, the never ending cycle of feeding and pooping, took every last iota of energy we had.

But despite the considerable demands, Emma turned out to be a gift in ways that I'd never anticipated. She took me out of my head, for one; forced me to stay present, and she renewed my sense of purpose at work.

And for that I was grateful.

Somehow three months slipped by, and then six— then almost a year. Overall, we had managed parenthood well enough, but sometimes I felt like a bystander in my own life, watching time race by like a subway train. Between fatherhood, supporting Megan through an extended interval of postpartum depression, and my promotion at Capital-Co., the goal of finishing my novel stalled.

Fortunately, my new full-time role paid much better, as I was given more responsibility as the Document Management Coordinator for the Compliance Department.

I learned all about task management and workflow, questionnaires and attestations, approvals and affirmations, personal trading, and case management.

But the best part was that I was finally out of the basement file room. I even got to sit near a window with a view. You don't realize how much you appreciate a view until you've stared at windowless walls in an underground room for the better part of a year. Besides, after being worried about finances for so many years, it was comforting to have benefits and a steady paycheck for a nice long stretch.

That stretch turned into three years, then four.

Alcohol helped me get through the fifth and sixth; I even started keeping a bottle of whiskey in my drawer at work. I started to wonder if I had become infected like my father, and his father before him.

I realize now that zombies do exist in real life. At work I see them shuffle through the halls like disconsolate mourners at a funeral that never ends. And every day at the office I struggle to keep the infection at bay. But the allure of security is like a velvet covered cage.

I cling to the hope of finishing my novel; it is my life. I have explained this to Megan many times. At first she seemed empathetic. But when I speak about my writing career now, her eyes seem to glaze over, and her speech takes on a slightly patronizing tone.

Yet she always seems to have just the right words to say when the job becomes unbearable, especially when I speak of quitting–which is often. She does her best–often with great fervor–to help me understand the importance of a steady paycheck. And she even rejoiced at my promotion to Senior Manager.

~

Megan never went back to acting, choosing instead to be a stay-at-home mom with some vague talk of starting her own business. This made sense the first few years as we were able to save a lot of money on day care. But now with Emma in school full-time, I often wonder what she does all day. Sometimes when I come home I smell the faint but musky scent of men's cologne in her hair.

Last month I confronted her about going back to acting, or at least investigating a part-time job. She cried hysterically and told me that I was being insensitive to her bouts of depression. It was a convincing performance, I admit. But, of course, Megan has a whole wall of trophies and ribbons that attest to her acting ability.

I think of my father wanting to protect me from the footlocker's contents. I wonder why he couldn't bring himself to destroy the manuscript; perhaps because it would have been like destroying the last glimmer of his own dream.

And still the nightmares come; I wander lost through some endless limbo where the ravaged faces of the infected stare at me through the darkness and shriek my name. Each time I must fight for my life against my father and grandfather, who reach out to drag me in.

But that isn't what wakes me up in terror night after night. What frightens me most is the familiar face that has joined the ranks of the infected, screaming and calling out my name.

The face of the woman I love.

WHISPERS IN THE TREES, SCREAMS IN THE DARK

A GHOSTLY HAZE shrouded the forest path, swallowing Blake up to his knees as he trudged deeper into the wilderness. He drew his red hood close about his face against the chill of the night, wishing to God he had more sensible winter clothes. But as a recent transplant from Los Angeles, a hooded sweatshirt was the warmest thing he owned.

The ambient moon and starlight proved no match for the inescapable gloom, and Blake was grateful that he'd been able to find a flashlight in his dad's toolbox. He raised it to get a look at the terrain ahead and caught glimpses of brilliant eyes watching him from the safety of the shadows. Creatures sang, the wind whispered through the trees, and something eerie-sounding—possibly an owl—called out.

He swung his flashlight back and forth across a maze of shadowy trunks.

The wind unnerved him the most. It seemed to give unholy life to the forest: sighs, heaves and exhalations from the trees—soft murmurs amongst the leaves. He reached into his sweatshirt pocket and withdrew a now chilled can of spray paint that he'd plundered from his dad's collection. After a few quick shakes of the can, he sprayed a conspicuous white "X" across a particularly thick trunk facing the forest path.

He'd gotten the idea from the story of *Hansel and Gretel*, but figured that white spray paint would be a heck of lot easier to locate on the way back than a trail of breadcrumbs.

He wiped mist from the face of his watch and strained to see the time. It was ten to midnight. He had ten minutes to reach the crossroads, where he'd find an old signpost with directions to the various hiking trails. At least, that's what Rusty and Seth had told him.

He hoped to God they wouldn't show up. Then he could turn around and head for home sweet home.

Well, that wasn't exactly true. Home had become anything but sweet since . . . *she* had soured it. How ironic that the first word that came to mind when he thought of Myra—his future stepmother—was *wicked*.

At first, he'd been thrilled to meet her. She'd managed to bring his dad out of the impenetrable shell he built around himself. But before long, she became his father's singular interest and Blake an afterthought. His father lavished Myra with a constant stream of gifts and fawned over her ceaselessly. And while she didn't live with them yet, Blake dreaded the inevitability of her taking up residence. But Dad was old fashioned about things, and claimed that it wouldn't be proper for them to live together until after their marriage in the spring.

Blake smirked at the thought. While it wasn't *proper* to live together before marriage, apparently it was just fine to hump like wild rabbits during those terribly awkward nights when Myra stayed over (and tried unsuccessfully to sneak out unseen in the morning).

Hearing his dad and future stepmother *doing it* hadn't been as traumatizing as Blake would have imagined. No, what had disturbed him—scratch that—*shamed* him to no end was the fact that hearing their moans, groans and passionate screams through the walls had aroused him.

After all, despite Myra's glacial attitude toward him, Blake had to admit she was hot for a woman of thirty-two. Hot enough to make a lonely dad forget his pain and help a fourteen year-old boy to take care of business under his sheets on more than one degrading night.

He imagined her then, naked and glistening on his father's sheets, her long legs spread out for him as he . . .

No!

Blake pushed the thought away. It was a lot more comfortable resenting her.

Thanks to Myra, he'd been torn away from the handful of friends he'd struggled to maintain back in sunny California. Thanks to her, he'd been dragged across three states and dropped smack into the bleak winter of Shitsville, Colorado, a town so remote you couldn't find a decent movie theater or shopping mall in less than an hour's drive. And while Blake's love for his father was unquestionable, he didn't think he could ever forgive him for the loss of his friends.

They were now as distant as his former grade school friends had become; friends that abandoned him after the summer his mother died; when he binged on food, soda and candy ceaselessly to try and forget the pain. It was the year he went from not terribly popular to a pariah when his classmates saw how much weight he'd gained.

These days, friends—even gimps and stutterers like Rusty and Seth—had been hard to come by. And it was that troubling thought that kept Blake pushing along the path, continuing deeper into the bowels of the forest, trying to ignore the wind as it whispered a low, lingering note, like a threatening invitation.

Blake crested a steep, mist-covered hill and spotted the crossroads signpost just ahead. He glanced back at his watch. Midnight.

Blake's teeth began to chatter from the cold, and he told himself he would wait no more than five minutes.

The forest encroached on the crossroads with its night clamor—the chirruping of crickets, the duck-like quacking sounds of wood frogs, the occasional screech of an owl. But one by one the forest voices faded and died until all that remained was the lonely sound of the signpost shingles creaking in the wind.

Blake raised his watch: five past midnight.

They've chickened out, he thought. *Thank God.*

He tightened his hood and headed back home.

Clouds gathered like a formation of dark soldiers, engulfing the moon. The forest was thrown into an impenetrable blackness. Even Blake's flashlight seemed to give up in exasperation.

He was suddenly grateful he'd had the foresight to spray white paint on landmarks along the path.

Was that the wind he heard? Or was something pushing through the foliage?

It grew louder.

Slithering. Something was . . . slithering.

It sounded like a snake moving swiftly through a field of dead leaves; a snake the size of a pickup truck.

It was close now.

Right behind . . . ?

Blake stood paralyzed. Even the trees seemed to hold their breath.

Something powerful brushed against the back of his legs, nearly bowling him over.

Blake was unable to make out any details, he was too

busy running for his life. He might have run all night and into the morning, but a fallen log caught his foot and ended the marathon.

He lay there, frozen in terror—unable to see anything in the crushing darkness.

The forest seemed to sense this, for he could hear its faint, mocking laughter—carried on bone-chilling winds.

As agonizing seconds ticked by, he imagined the shape of a hundred-foot snake coiled before him, fangs as long as yard sticks, dripping with venom—waiting to strike.

But the clouds parted and there was only the moon, the stars and the endless forest.

After a thorough scan of the immediate area, Blake allowed himself to breathe again—but only just. While the monstrous snake couldn't be seen, simply knowing it was out there made his chest hurt. How strange, he thought, that it had appeared at the moment he'd decided to leave the forest.

Then he heard it again: faint laughter. This time it was distinct enough to know it wasn't the forest. Nervously, he glanced over his shoulder and spotted Seth's tall, lumbering figure in the distance, followed by Rusty, who—as usual— hobbled several feet behind. They didn't seem to notice him, though. They were too busy gabbing and chortling as they trudged along the narrow path, seemingly without a care in the world. Their lanterns danced like two giant fireflies in the night.

Blake had never been so happy to see two morons in his life.

~

Blake decided not to mention his encounter with the colossal, man-eating snake—or *whatever* it was. He knew

Rusty and Seth would just scoff and call him a *wussy*. When he caught them glancing curiously at the small gash in his forehead, he mentioned falling—but skipped the details. They didn't seem to care enough to pursue it, and by the time they had walked a quarter mile deeper into the forest, it had clearly been forgotten.

But the touch of the loathsome thing still lingered: phantom scales gliding across his legs, so icy he could feel them through his jeans—a sense memory that refused to go away.

"Hurry up, chubby," Rusty called back at Blake, walking a goosestep with his bad left leg. He and Seth were about fifteen feet ahead of him on the path. "You're the only freakin' kid I know slower than me!"

Seth snickered at that. "Huh-he's just st-stallin', man. Afraid he's guh-gonna luh-lose the bet."

Blake glanced away. He didn't want them to see the hurt in his eyes. He couldn't show any weakness with these two. Instead, he simply muttered "Whatever, dude," and gave them a dismissive wave.

The bets between them had become such a tedious ritual since he'd moved into the neighborhood, part of an unspoken but compulsory initiation into Rusty and Seth's exclusive club of two.

But this bet wasn't like their usual nonsense. Like when he bet Seth that he could hold his breath the longest and had won a *Playboy* magazine that Seth had stolen from his dad's stash; or when Rusty won five whole dollars off Blake by betting him that the Hulk was stronger than Superman.

Blake had demanded proof, of course, so Rusty had produced a comic book that explained that the angrier the Hulk got, the stronger he got; which in theory, meant that there was no limit to the Hulk's strength. Therefore, if the

Hulk got angry enough he was stronger than anyone—even the big blue Boy Scout.

The stakes on those bets had been relatively low. Tonight's wager was a different matter entirely.

According to Rusty and Seth (who both tended to stretch, bend, and occasionally break the truth in half), there was a drop dead gorgeous girl, perhaps eighteen or nineteen years old, who lived in a broken down house deep in the woods. As they told it, each time they went to visit the house, she would give them a full striptease through her window. Oh, and to top it off, she made every Playmate of the Month look like rotted dog meat.

Blake told them that they were full of crap, so of course they had bet him that he was wrong. So wrong, in fact, they were willing to bet each of their video game consoles. Blake knew he'd lose their respect if he backed down at that point, so he'd foolishly bet the only thing he had of real worth: his comic book collection.

He had never evaluated the fiscal worth of his collection, but he knew its personal value; it was priceless. Comics were a lot more than funny books to him. They were his private travel guide through a multidimensional universe of possibilities; a place where a fourteen-year-old boy didn't have to think about diabetes and obesity, or watch helplessly as his mother is eaten away by cancer. In the dark days after his mother's death, the colorful heroes and villains were the only things he could still believe in, because no matter how bad things got, the good guys always won in the end. Oh yes, his comic collection meant everything to him, and now thanks to his big fat mouth, he'd risked it all.

God help him, but he'd come too far to back out now.

One by one, each of the boys entered what looked like a shallow cave made entirely of branches and leaves. When they stepped through to the other side, it was as though they had been transported into a primeval landscape. Towering trees stood like dark sentries, seeming to lean forward as the three walked past, curious as to who would dare trespass on their strange and dangerous territory.

"How much farther is this imaginary house?" Blake said, trying to keep the quiver from his voice.

Rusty turned to face him, his mouth gaping in a kind of threatening rictus. "Wussy . . . wussy . . . wuuusssy . . . "

Seth laughed like a hyena.

Blake felt his face flush. *Wussy:* the dreaded five-letter word. Rusty was adept at picking at Blake's most sensitive scabs.

Blake hugged himself. He knew his membership status was teetering on a precipice. To be branded with the "W" word meant losing all the ground he'd gained in the past few weeks.

He glanced nervously at the labyrinthine forest.

The looming trees seemed to stare back.

More than ever he wanted to extricate himself from the situation, but he didn't see any way out.

Rusty rolled his eyes dismissively and resumed hobbling along the path. "C'mon ya big fat lard ass, it's not much farther."

Seth bobbed his head in agreement and shambled after Rusty.

Blake watched as a towering patch of wild grass seemed to devour the two boys.

If he tried to head back home now, he'd not only lose the bet by default, he might have to face that . . . *thing* out in the forest again.

Alone.

A moment later, he was racing like hell to catch up with the gimp and the oaf.

Blake didn't take his eyes off Rusty and Seth as he pursued them. Self-loathing pecked at him as he watched them twist and wind their way through the dense foliage just ahead. It was astonishing how desperate he'd become for friends.

Blake pushed and shoved his way through a particularly dense thicket. He wondered if their wild claim held any truth. It was too far-fetched: a beautiful blonde girl living in the middle of the forest, who stripped naked for schoolboys? Neither Rusty nor Seth could provide a plausible explanation: Lonely? Horny? Psychotic? It didn't matter to them as long as she was willing.

According to their story, they'd discovered her house late one night after venturing onto a secluded strip of private property. She had been standing half-naked in the second story window, brushing her golden locks. When she eventually spotted them she didn't bother to cover herself up. To their surprise and delight, she gave them a titillating striptease—including a steamy finale that included a peek at her holiest of holies.

Blake considered their story with a thin smirk. The more likely version was that they had snuck onto the property, peeked into the poor girl's bedroom window, caught her in her undies—and embellished the rest.

A strip show? He couldn't help but chuckle. *For those two morons?*

"No way," he consoled himself in the darkness, keeping the hope alive that he'd win the bet.

As they topped the last of a series of rolling hills, the house appeared like a specter through a light veil of rippling fog. From the Victorian era, the two-storied structure was a study in contrasts: while its design was large and opulent, obvious neglect had given it a ramshackle appearance.

It boasted a large dome on the west side and a tall conical turret on the east, which gave it a fairytale-like aspect. Wild grass and clusters of weeds taller than the boys overran a sizable garden in the front. The dilapidated front porch was a large façade entangled with creeping vines. But the most eye-catching feature of the house was the eclectic mix of window shapes, the two largest fitted with red-stained glass. They stared out from the darkness like monstrous, bloodshot eyes.

The boys stood in the dead garden, gazing up at the turret's tall central window. Blake found it hard to believe that anyone, much less the beautiful girl Rusty and Seth had described, would live in such decay. "Looks like no one's home," he said, cringing at the desperation in his voice.

Rusty gave a Cheshire Cat grin. "Relax. She's always here. I don't think she ever leaves."

Seth, as usual, nodded in agreement.

Rusty picked up a small stone and heaved it at the turret, careful to avoid the window. Blake winced at the dull *thunk*.

Though he was eager to win the bet, a deeper part of him secretly wished that the gimp and the oaf were telling the truth. After all, seeing a real naked woman was the next evolutionary step toward manhood. Sure, he'd seen boobies and private parts before, in magazines and on the Web, but he'd never seen a live nude girl before.

Suddenly, it dawned on him what such a woman, if she actually existed, could do for his standing with the other boys at school. His mind began to churn with possibilities. If by some miracle she actually stripped on demand, could he not use that to his advantage? The gimp and the oaf didn't have any special claim over her. And once word got around that Blake Hennessy could provide access to a free peep show, he'd have friends lining up outside his door.

Then he could cut loose the two morons standing next to him.

As if on cue, Seth glanced over with an idiotic grin. Blake grinned back—though for reasons entirely his own.

In the window, a silhouette appeared. It was so sudden that Blake leapt back a step, his heart fighting to catch up.

"Is . . . that her?"

The two boys nodded in unison, never taking their eyes off the dark figure.

The turret window was easily six feet tall, more than enough to get a full view of the figure standing there. But the darkness and red-flecked glass made it difficult to make out any detail.

Blake turned to Rusty, his eyes scrunched with frustration. "I can't see anything."

Rusty winked and gestured for him to follow. "C'mon, you want a front row seat for this."

Seth followed Rusty and Blake followed Seth as they moved closer to the dilapidated house. They came to a halt just feet from the turret wall, gazing straight up.

Blake's desire to win the bet was suddenly overshadowed by his desire to see the woman in the window. He didn't understand why or how, but something told him that tonight would forever change his life.

A silvery light came on from somewhere inside the room; it illuminated both the stained glass and the devastating beauty behind it. Blake felt as if he'd been kicked in the stomach—she was breathtaking.

Gracefully, she moved closer to the window. She wore nothing but a skimpy, silken slip. Blake could feel his Adam's apple drying in his throat. She was everything the boys had described and more: an impossibly perfect face; full, sultry lips; exotic eyes that glistened in the light; and all of it framed by golden, ankle-length hair that seemed to move with a life of its own. The abstract touches of red color in the stained glass accented her magical allure.

Suddenly, Blake had feelings that he hadn't known existed: sexual yes, but not of the usual raging hormonal kind; these were filtered through a prism of indefinable emotional longing.

And they were relentless.

The blonde seductress stared straight ahead—out past the dense woods and into the starry night. Did she really not see them or was this all part of the act? Blake had no idea. But as she delicately drew a brush through her cascading locks, he was reminded of Rapunzel trapped in the tower. How wonderful, he thought, to be the prince that would save her.

Stroke after stroke the three boys watched gape-mouthed as she brushed, her body moving in a gentle dance of artful seduction. Finally, Rusty spoke: "Somebody owes us his comic collection."

It took Blake a moment to readjust his thoughts. He'd been so preoccupied with his schoolboy fantasies that he'd forgotten all about the stupid bet. Yet, impressed as he was, he wasn't ready to part with his most cherished possession. "No way," he said. "The bet was that she'd strip *naked.*"

Rusty was about to retort angrily when—as if in answer—the blonde goddess let the straps fall from her shoulders one by one—revealing herself completely. Rusty's smile spread across his face like melted wax. The woman's shape was sublime. And yet, for some inexplicable reason, Blake found himself fixated on her eyes. They were irresistible; insatiable.

She didn't blink. Neither did he. A sultry smile formed around the edges of her mouth—he felt his lips comply.

Seth watched the seemingly intimate exchange between Blake and the girl and gasped in awe.

Rusty turned to Blake with a suspicious look. "What the hell dude, you know this girl or something?"

Blake shook his head *no*, although at that moment he felt as if he'd known her all his life. It was as if she'd been plucked from his imagination and transported behind the window: the embodiment of everything he'd ever fantasized about.

He would have remained content to watch her from amongst the dead tangles of the garden forever.

But fantasy was abruptly shattered by reality. Blake watched, dumbfounded, as the woman raised her index finger and gave him a *come hither* gesture—beckoning him inside the house.

Rusty's eyes looked as wide as saucers. "Holy—did you see that? The wussy's got game!"

Seth's hyena laughter was unbridled, "Sh-she . . . wuh-wants . . . the wuh-wussy!" Rusty joined in, embracing the hilarity of it.

Blake wasn't laughing though. The world had suddenly spun off its axis and plunged him into zero gravity. His mind reeled at the implications. He hadn't so much as kissed a girl, much less . . .

Blake found himself choking for air. He heard himself squeak, "I—I can't . . . "

Rusty and Seth did a double take, staring at him as if he'd suddenly grown a second head.

Blake didn't notice. He was still fixated on the blonde goddess, feeling the entire weight of the universe upon him. She was indeed beckoning him—but for what? What would they *do* up there? What would he possibly say to a woman who could have any man she wanted? He knew he'd just wind up embarrassing himself.

No, he decided. It was far safer to stand below her window. From here he could watch and fantasize about saving her from the great evils of the world, from jerks like the gimp and the oaf, or worse—like the monstrous snake that lived in the woods.

At least in fantasies, he thought, the hero never fails.

The woman seemed to sense his insecurity. She gave him a warm, compassionate smile—then floated away from the window, disappearing into the shadows.

His heart began to ache.

Seth grabbed him by the arm. "Guh-go . . . you guh-gotta go . . ."

"But—" Blake shuddered.

Rusty's face was pinched with disgust. "But *what?* You want us to tell everyone what a big faggot you are?"

Blake shuddered at the thought. Tonight was clearly his final test. He'd already lost his comic collection. Now he risked losing his only friends, too. If he backed out now, they'd make him the laughing stock of his entire class. He'd be a pariah again, just like back in grade school. Suddenly his dream of lining up friends for a striptease in the woods had transformed into a nightmare.

"Wussy, wussy, wuuuuussy," Rusty chanted with relish.

Blake's emotions and logic waged war. He measured the terrifying proposition of entering the house against the horror of being taunted and ostracized by a hundred or so of his peers.

In the end, there was really no choice at all.

"I'll go," he murmured.

Seth yelped his approval and slapped Blake on the back, surprising him with an openly affectionate gesture. It gave him the courage to move his thousand pound feet toward the house.

By the time he'd reached the front door, his heart was pounding so hard he could scarcely hear the boy's hoots and hollers from behind. When he'd found the nerve to open it and peek inside, the blood rushed so loudly through his ears that he couldn't hear himself think.

Inside, the house was pitch black.

Nervously, he glanced back over his shoulder: Rusty and Seth watched from the edge of the dead garden, cheering him on with lewd sexual gestures.

He'd make them pay for putting him through this. He didn't know how yet—but he'd find a way. The resolution was cold comfort as he stepped into the silent house— swallowed by the pall of darkness.

He stood in the foyer for a moment, letting his eyes adjust. He swung his flashlight around, swirls of dust wafting across the single beam of light.

The only other illumination emanated from outside, where ghosts of moonlight drifted in through a window in the drawing room. Blake grimaced, unsettled by the fact that there were no lights on. He felt as vulnerable as he was back in the woods alone—perhaps even more so.

He pulled down his red hood and croaked, "Hello? It's me, Blake . . . from outside."

Idiot. As if she didn't know.

The house ate his shallow voice; the feebleness of it made him cringe. He wondered if the woman in the window would find it as distasteful. Hesitantly, he took a few steps into the musty space—past a looming Grandfather clock with a shattered face, its gears frozen in time.

He stepped down into the drawing room, where he could make out an ornate table, its marble top layered with what looked like decades of dust. Around it was a smattering of expensive looking furniture, a floor lamp with a missing shade, and a small parlor set covered in webs from spiders that had abandoned them an eternity ago.

He recoiled at the snarling head of a large, grey wolf—a hunting trophy—protruding from the wall above a fireplace. It seemed to stare right through him with soulless, unblinking eyes. *You're in the wrong place, little boy*, the wolf seemed to say. *This house is for dead things.*

Blake gulped audibly, averting his eyes. Something didn't connect here. What kind of person would live in such a ghastly state? It was as if the house was decomposing before his eyes.

Was the woman upstairs imprisoned here? And if so—by whom? His thoughts flashed again to the thing living in the woods. He recalled a great dragon-like monster from a book that had captured his imagination as a small boy. The beast watched over a beautiful princess held captive in an ancient castle and devoured any interlopers that dared to enter its forest dominion.

Unsettled by the thought, Blake played his flashlight over the walls, thankful for its meager luminance. Suddenly, there was a slam from upstairs and Blake jumped. A door seized by the wind, or perhaps a heavy piece of furniture thrown against a wall?

A wooden floorboard above him creaked as if in pain.

Blake seized up, paralyzed with fear. When the second creak came, he nearly ran for the front door.

And then her voice called out; a chill lanced through him and, yet, its timbre also warmed his heart. It was soft; impossibly sultry, and it emanated from a shadowy landing to his right. A silvery light leaked faintly onto the second floor; perhaps the same light that had surrounded the ethereal woman at the window?

The incorporeal voice called out again: a mystical aria that carried him through the shadows and up past the landing. He glanced toward the top of the stairs and caught a glimpse of golden hair before it disappeared into the shadows.

Sweat had collected under his arms, though the house was as cold as a meat locker. His mind raced as he stood at the invisible line between safety and the unknown. The top of the stairs represented a threshold: perhaps to danger, but more likely—and more importantly—to a different status amongst his peers.

It was that intense desire that drove him up one step . . . then another: each footfall creaking louder than the last.

The corridor was empty, save for the reflection of a thickset, pale-faced boy in the hall mirror at the top of the stairs. A small, iron wall sconce provided the cold silvery light he had spied from below. There were three doors ahead: one to his left, one to his right, and another facing him at the end of the hallway.

The door to his left was slightly ajar.

Waiting.

Blake's nostrils flared. A heavy scent—spices perhaps— invaded his lungs as he crept toward the door. His long shadow stretched—then melded into the darkness that lay ahead.

A few more faltering steps and the weathered-looking door opened silently before him, as if attended by some ghostly concierge.

"Hello . . ." he whispered into the black hole of a room.

The only answer was the low, creeping wind moaning from outside.

Tentatively, he stepped inside. Crouched against the far wall as if ready to strike, was a large beast of a bed.

Next to it, standing motionless, silent and half hidden in shadow, was the woman he'd seen in the window. Her back was turned toward him, so that all he could see was the waterfall of blonde hair that flowed over her shoulders to the backs of her bare feet. She was staring at herself in a full-length mirror that adorned the face of an ornately carved wardrobe.

Who's the fairest of them all? a crazed voice said in Blake's mind.

He aimed his flashlight at the mirror and what he saw reflected there made his eyes widen in horror.

Her skin was incongruous: creamy and beautiful in some areas, horribly mottled and scaled in others—as if she were half human and half snake. Her long hair hung like a curtain, obscuring her features . . . except for her unblinking, lidless eyes. They looked like two eggshells in the darkness, pupilless and white.

Her breathing came out like a hiss.

As Blake gazed upon her nightmarish reflection, a knife of icy terror impaled his heart, and a whimper of fear escaped his throat.

Her head snapped toward him violently, hair flying with wild fury. A hideous forked tongue erupted from between her lips and tasted the air.

Blake stumbled back and felt urine spill from him in a steady stream.

She moved closer, but he was already running. He managed to hook his fingers around the doorknob and slam the door behind him. He was about to make a dash for the stairs, but somehow, inconceivably . . . they had moved. They were easily twenty yards further away and seemed to stretch as he moved toward them, as if viewed through a funhouse mirror at a carnival. An optical illusion, or . . . ?

The door behind him flung open with such force it was torn from its hinges. Blake didn't have time to think . . . only act. He'd never make the stairs, so he sprinted the other way, to the door at the other end of the hall, which appeared much closer.

Please be unlocked, Oh GOD . . . please be unlocked!

He reached the door in seconds, shoved it open with this shoulder, slammed it shut behind him, and threw all of his weight against it. The knob had an old brass turn lock and he fumbled with it . . . screamed at it . . . then managed to lock it, losing his grip on his flashlight in the process.

It clattered on the hardwood floor and faded. Frantically, he scooped it back up, smacking it against his hand. But it had gone as dead as the eyes of the thing beyond the door. There was a dim source of illumination in the room and he turned to look, grateful for the shafts of moonlight that filtered through a tall window.

Flies buzzed in every direction. A dark cloud of them swarmed him and he had to keep his lips shut to keep them from infesting his mouth. His eyes darted around the enormous room in the hopes of an escape route. But there were no doors, except the one through which he'd entered. The only other way out was through the six-foot-tall, stained-glass window directly across from him. He thought of Rusty and Seth and prayed that they were in the same spot. Perhaps he could signal for help. Either way, he decided right then and there that he'd leap through the glass if it came down to it; anything would be better than facing that thing again.

He swatted at the relentless assault of flies and ran toward the window. His eyes caught something lurking just ahead. It was bulky and expelled wet, gurgling noises. The whole room was permeated with its putrid, spicy scent.

Blake's eyes began to adjust to the darkness and the unmoving thing took shape: it was a huge iron vat, perhaps six feet around. There was no discernible fire, yet the contents seethed and hissed.

His legs trembled so badly he could hardly control them. He knew if the thing in the hallway wanted in, it could reduce the door to splinters. For the briefest of moments he wondered if it had left the house, perhaps finding Rusty and Seth easier targets.

But then from behind the door, he heard the scratching of fingers, and the floorboards complained as a great weight moved across them.

Then, there was silence.

Blake braced himself.

A moan rose from somewhere inside the room.

Blake spun to face the darkest corner.

Straining his eyes, he could just make out the outline of a tall figure sitting in a chair facing him, unmoving.

"Blake . . ." a familiar voice rasped.

He recognized it immediately.

"Dad?"

He moved closer and saw that his father was naked, sitting in a heavy looking high-backed chair. His wrists and ankles were bound with thick rope; thin rivulets of blood seeped from beneath. He was pale and anemic, as if every ounce of life had been drained from his body.

"It'll be okay . . ." he murmured, his eyes glazed and distant. His chin dropped to his chest, as if he didn't have the strength to hold it up.

Blake rushed to him and tugged at the ropes. They hardly budged. It would take time to untie them—time they didn't have.

"What are you doing here?" Blake demanded. "What is that . . . *thing* out there?"

"She . . . " his father coughed horribly. "She makes the pain go away . . . "

And then he was gone.

Blake grabbed his father by the shoulders and shook him, pleading. "Dad! No! I need you . . . please!"

But his father's head just lolled to one side, life drained away.

Tears spilled from Blake's eyes. There was nothing he could do for his father. His only option now was to try and escape. He stood up and prepared to jump through the window. He'd probably die from the fall, but at least it would be quick.

The door creaked and Blake glanced nervously at it; a pool of blackness was seeping into the room from underneath. The shadows in the room came alive. They slinked along the walls and crawled across the floor—surrounding him like a black carpet of spiders. The sight of it immobilized him with fear; he watched as the oozing darkness began to take shape . . . a familiar shape.

Before him stood the naked, voluptuous form of Myra.

At first he blinked in disbelief, but then the cogs of his mind began to turn, faster . . . and faster still, questions and answers beginning to connect, like some mad jigsaw puzzle. Like how his father—a balding and pudgy traveling salesman—could have landed such a beauty as Myra: the kind of woman who could have anyone she wanted.

Sure he had lavished her with gifts and attention, but it had never seemed right——the love never real. It was clear now that she had never intended to marry his father; the only thing Myra had wanted was to suck the life right out of him.

The woman grinned at Blake as if it had been carved into her face with a straight razor. The lower half of her body began to twist and coil impossibly, like some kind of monstrous snake, and Blake realized that she was the same creature that had brushed against him in the forest.

He tried to scream, but the sound couldn't escape. He staggered back as she slithered toward him. There was relentless hunger in her eyes. Watching her, he could see that her beauty was an illusion: she was old, perhaps as old as time itself.

They locked eyes. Predator and prey: each moving in a circle around the dusky room. Blake barely avoided the gurgling pot, but didn't notice the pile of human bones next to it. He tripped over the maggot-infested remains of a child's skull and fell face down onto a cold mound of flesh, bones and human refuse.

His body convulsed with a dry retch as his mind flashed to something he'd overheard one morning on his dad's battered old radio: a random broadcast about a handful of missing children in the area.

He scrambled to his feet, chest heaving. But as he faced the woman again, the ravenousness seemed to drain from her. She was changing again. Her eyes began to soften with what looked like genuine compassion. Her hair swirled around her as if alive and transmuted from auburn to a familiar brunette.

His mother stood before him.

Her bare arms reached out invitingly; her delicate hands outstretched. It was impossible. A cruel illusion. And yet Blake felt his fear melt away as if by magic. His mother smiled at him warmly.

He found himself moving closer to her, as if by a force not his own.

He wasn't scared anymore. Everything had become

crystal clear: this woman understood him. Loved him. And she would take his pain away.

He would never have to be lonely. He would never have to worry about being an outcast. He would never again feel that terrible emptiness that could never be filled.

She would remove all of it forever.

A voice whispered inside his head. *This was always about you—not your father. You're the special one. You're the one who has what I need.*

Blake raised his arms to embrace her.

She held him tightly against her bosom and her fingers pressed into the thick meat of his back. It was an odd sensation, as if her fingers were sharp and claw-like.

But he didn't mind. For that exquisite, timeless moment, Blake Hennessy knew peace.

***

Rusty and Seth had stared at the turret window for what seemed like hours, grateful when the sounds of terror and mayhem finally stopped. To them, the screaming was always the worst part.

A penetrating gust of wind arose, as a silent figure stepped from the darkness; neither boy noticed until it was looming right over them.

They spun to face it, faces blanched by the light of the watchful moon.

Rusty somehow drew the courage to speak. "We . . . did good? Lots of meat on that kid."

A hint of a smile curved the silent figure's lips.

"Please . . . " Rusty fought back tears. "Will you lift your curse now? My leg . . . it's almost eaten away."

"Yuh . . . yeah . . . " Seth dared to add. "And . . . I cuh-can't . . . buh-barely . . . talk no . . . muh-more."

The figure placed firm hands on each of the terrified boys' shoulders. With a voice as cold as a grave in winter, she rasped, "My beauty . . . requires renewal."

"But . . . how many more?" Rusty pleaded as the tears finally came.

The succubus-witch-thing only cackled, caressing the youthful suppleness of her face and relishing the patchwork of newly acquired flesh.

INTRUDERS

MASON'S HANDS STILL trembled, though not as badly as when he'd arrived a half-hour earlier.

Sara hadn't experienced this side of him during the two years they had been lovers. Though it unnerved her, she did her best not to show it.

"Are you okay to talk now?" she said.

"I think so," he said, his voice still shaky. "Can I get a refill?"

"Of course." Sara took the empty ceramic cup from him. It was his third coffee so far, mixed with a touch of Amaretto to take off the edge.

Sara moved about her well-organized kitchen, her mind racing with questions. Why in the world would Mason show up five years after falling off the face of the earth? And of all the places in the world to hide out, why pick *her* apartment? Most importantly, who was chasing him? And what did he expect her to do about it?

She reentered the living room balancing an overfull cup, and noticed Mason lying back on the couch. He ran his fingers through his thick, wavy hair and she remembered how he always did that after a great lovemaking session; she felt her cheeks grow warm at the thought.

Mason always had that effect on her. And despite the

fact that he was narcissistic, noncommittal, and could have won an award for world's worst boyfriend, he was the best sex partner she'd ever had.

"Thank you," he said. She could tell he meant it. There was a refreshing vulnerability in his eyes that made him more attractive—if that was humanly possible.

"All right," Sara said with a deep exhalation. "You want to tell me what's going on?"

Mason sat up and took the coffee. "You'll think I've lost my mind."

"Says the guy at my door at three in the morning screaming for his life." She was trying to lighten the situation, but it wasn't working.

She sat down close to him on the leather couch and put her hand on top of his. It was warm, and his skin was still as soft as she remembered. "Sorry. You know I make bad jokes when I'm scared."

"You *should* be scared."

"Of what?

"Of . . . *things.*"

Sara scowled, not sure where this could possibly be going.

"The kind of things that can drive a person mad."

"I'm sorry, I don't . . . "

"Of course you don't. You have no context." He took a measured sip of coffee and continued, "I don't have all the answers. But I can tell you what I know. I owe you that much."

Sara took a deep breath, wondering what he could really owe her after all this time. "Should I make myself a drink?"

"Not a bad idea."

Sara made a beeline for the bar on the other side of the living room. She definitely needed a drink.

Mason cleared his throat and said, "I started researching a new book about a year and a half ago, called *The Madness Within*."

Mason's writing career had taken off like a rocket not long after he broke up with her. More salt in the wound.

"I was commissioned to write a true crime book, and I interviewed several serial killers in prison."

Sarah mixed a healthy dose of rum into a glass of Coke. "Serial killers? Jesus. Like who?"

"Remember Ned Hawson, the Headhunter?"

Sara sat down in the loveseat facing Mason, her interest piqued. "Sure. You actually went into the same room with a guy who collected heads?"

"He was behind prison glass—I was perfectly safe."

Sara shivered at the thought. "You couldn't get me in the same building with that freak, much less the same room. Who else?"

"Richard Nakamura. He was the guy in Toledo who ate the tongues of his victims. There were several more after that who weren't as famous, but they were just as interesting. Anyway, it wasn't long before I started to notice a strange pattern during these interviews. It took my book in an unexpected direction."

"A pattern?"

"They all heard voices. Y'know, like David Berkowitz?"

She didn't recognize the name.

"Son of Sam? Never mind—before your time." Mason sat forward, his eyes narrowed. "Anyway, all of them claimed that . . . 'voices' were responsible for their actions. Some said it was God, others said it was the devil. Some believed it was the voices of their victims, and one of them was convinced they came from another dimension. All of them were diagnosed schizophrenic.

"Of the group, Nakamura was the most lucid and intelligent. I was the only person he'd ever agreed to meet with. And that was only because I'd written him a letter telling him that I believed the voices were real.

"We met on several occasions. Fascinating guy; he was a former psychiatrist who spent much of his career working with schizophrenic criminals himself. Ultimately, he felt that his condition was the result of long-term exposure to his own patients."

Sara said, "You mean . . . as in he thought the disorder was contagious?"

"In a way yes, sort of like a virus. A *mind virus*. Nakamura told me that the victim must be susceptible to be affected. Which I thought was strange, since he was a doctor who specialized in mental disorders. But he explained that his natural skepticism—that is, his immunity—had been weakened after so many years."

"But a disorder is not a disease . . . immunity to what?"

"The truth. You see, not long after my initial interviews, I started to hear the voices, too."

Sara nearly dropped her drink. She caught herself staring at Mason in horror, immediately adjusted to neutral, and hoped he hadn't noticed. When he'd first arrived, she'd been terrified of who might be chasing him. But suddenly she was keenly aware of her vulnerability. If Mason had indeed lost his mind, she could be in serious trouble.

Her eyes drifted over to the rack on the kitchen counter that held her cutlery, and a meat mallet. She took note of the biggest and sharpest of the knives.

Mason's eyes seemed to look right through her. "I know you don't believe me. You've always been a natural skeptic. I remember struggling to bring you from atheism to agnosticism—and failing miserably."

"If you're hearing voices, then there must be a perfectly logical explanation, Mason—some kind of chemical imbalance. It doesn't mean you're crazy. And I know some people that can help."

"Doctors can't help, Sara . . . because the voices *are* real. And they don't want me to finish my book and expose them to the public—they're not prepared for that kind of scrutiny yet. They're out there right now—looking for me. At this point, it doesn't even matter if I don't publish the book—they'll kill me simply because I know too much."

He downed the rest of his drink like a shot and buried his face in his hands.

Sara grimaced. Why was it always the most damaged men that attracted her? Her mother told her it was a compulsion to feel needed. And while she hated her for saying it, it was probably true.

Mason needed her help, and that was something she hadn't felt for a long time. Not since Bradley had dumped her two years ago, after she'd helped him through an ugly divorce and let him live with her, rent free, for six months. Once he'd gotten back on his feet, he repaid her by shacking up with a dirty whore half Sara's age.

And now Mason shows up on her doorstep, five years after kicking her to the curb. She loathed herself for the hint of satisfaction she felt knowing he'd chosen *her* apartment as a safe haven. Was it that far a stretch to believe that he had finally realized her worth after all?

Against her better judgment, she heard herself say, "Look, I'm sure there's an answer to all this—a logical explanation for whatever you're going through. Let me help you. I know a great doctor. He's easy to talk to and really helped me with my depression after the . . . well, he's really good."

Mason laughed, but his eyes remained serious. "Doctors can't help, Sara. Meds either. Believe me, I've tried every antipsychotic available. I've seen two psychiatrists and one well-known psychologist, too."

"You've been diagnosed with schizophrenia?"

"Of course. Do you think anyone in the medical profession would consider for one second that the voices are real?"

"No . . . I suppose not."

"It doesn't matter anyway. *I* know they're real. And they want me dead."

"Who? Who are *they*?"

Mason set his cup firmly on the coffee table. "Look . . . I don't think it's a good idea for me to tell you any more details. I never would've involved you in the first place, but they were chasing me, and, well . . . you were the only person I knew in this area."

Sara felt her chest tighten. "I see. So . . . I was just the most conveniently located ex-girlfriend."

"Sara, it's not like that. I was desperate—not thinking. I should go. If they find me here, you'll be in danger, too."

He started to get off the couch, but Sara stopped him with a gentle hand. "No, it's okay," she said. "I'm being childish. Please . . . forgive me."

Mason looked tired, the kind of tired that might kill a man if he went too much longer without sleep. He rubbed his stubbly jaw with his hand, as if trying to decide what to do, yet unable to come to a suitable conclusion.

"I want to help you," Sara said, a little more desperately than she'd intended. "Let me help you. I want to understand."

And that was true. She did want to understand. She wanted to know how a man such as Mason Tanner could have fallen so far. God help her, she genuinely wanted to understand.

A single teardrop rolled down his cheek and he quickly wiped it away. "I'm going to die soon—and the only thing people will remember about me is that I lost my mind."

"Mason, I can't pretend that I understand any of this, but I'm a good listener."

Mason looked into her eyes, and for a moment she saw them soften. "Yes," he said, "you were always were. I took a lot of things for granted back then."

Sara took his hand, held it firmly.

He said, "Honestly, if just one person I knew understood the truth . . . that would give me some peace."

Sara tightened her fingers around his. "I'm listening. Who is it you think wants to kill you?"

"Not who . . . what."

"Okay. What are we talking about then?" Sara said, trying not to sound patronizing.

"What they are *exactly* is debatable, but I can tell you what I know, based on the work of Richard Nakamura, who spent years doing his own research."

"The serial killer."

Mason sighed—as if anticipating her skepticism. "The research predates his psychotic break, back when he was still a renowned psychiatrist. He had taken extensive notes when it became clear that several of his schizophrenic patients were hearing the same types of voices. He was convinced these invisible beings were real and not from our world—not even from this plane of reality. On a quantum level, he believes their existence is of a different vibration, which is why they are almost imperceptible. Yet they've somehow found a way to intrude on our dimension."

Sara wasn't sure what was more disturbing, the things

Mason was saying or the conviction with which he said them. "And . . . what do you think they want?"

"To experiment and observe. The people who hear their voices—like me—we're part of a large control group—and it's growing. New York City is one of the focal points."

"Why here?" Sara continued to probe, hoping that if Mason discovered a flaw in his own logic the whole delusion might begin to unravel.

Mason rubbed his eyes as he spoke, "There are several hubs around the world: Cairo, Mumbai, Buenos Aires, Madrid, and New York—the noisiest cities in the world. The excessive sound pollution—traffic, sirens, alarms, jackhammers, crowds, and everything in between—covers their activities. The higher the baseline decibel level of a city, the better it masks their voices and communications, making it easier for them to hide in plain sight."

Mason leaned forward, looking deep into Sara's eyes. "Don't you get it? These *things* walk among us all day, every day, experimenting on us . . . studying the effects. But that's not the worst part: their test subjects kill or harm others, suffer from extreme schizophrenia, or eventually kill themselves to stop the voices. No one notices it here because people are used to seeing crazies wandering around New York."

Sara had to admit that his delusion was well thought out. And in some perverse way, she was intrigued at how deep the story went. "What kind of experiments are they doing?" she said.

"A form of mind control. They test our strengths and search for weaknesses."

"For what purpose?"

"To pit us against each other. It's strictly small scale for now—a testing phase—they don't want to draw too much attention. But eventually they'll be able to set entire countries against each other. And once that happens, they'll control everything."

"But why? To take over the world?"

"Look, I don't know exactly, Sara. I'm not privy to their agenda. But based on the work Nakamura did with his patients, and my own experiences hearing the voices, it wouldn't be that far a stretch to imagine an invasion of some kind."

"So, you actually hear these voices?"

Mason finished his drink with one last gulp. "I didn't hear them at first because I thought it was all bullshit. I just assumed that the killers I interviewed were indeed schizophrenic. But after extensive interviews with Nakamura, I began to see that there were too many coincidences, too many patterns that couldn't be denied. Nakamura is an intelligent, lucid man—and despite his homicidal tendencies, a charming fellow to boot. Over time, I gained his trust, and he confided things to me that he'd never shared with anyone else.

"He told me to start observing the 'crazies' in the city; you know, the ones that talk to themselves. Since the average person avoids them like the plague, this has given the intruders a false sense of security. He told me to get as close as I could. And eventually, the intruders would slip up and I would hear the voices, too.

"It wasn't long after that I started noticing people talking to themselves all over the city. They had always been around, of course, I just hadn't been attuned to it. There were a lot of homeless people, as you would expect, but I also saw everyday looking people, too. One day I'd see a man dressed in a business suit, waiting at the crosswalk, murmuring to himself, and the next I'd see someone yelling and screaming at invisible entities—having arguments with thin air.

"And then something happened on the subway that changed everything."

Mason seemed to look within himself, as if watching some invisible film being unspooled in his mind.

"There was this decrepit homeless woman on the train in a corner by herself. She wore a pair of filthy pajamas, and had wrapped herself in a tattered old blanket. Her hair was grey and wild and she was just crouched there, facing the corner. I couldn't quite make out her face. No one wanted to sit next to her—so I did.

"And I listened."

"Most of what she said seemed nonsensical at first, end of the world stuff mostly. Something about an 'invasion' and how God had forsaken her. I'd heard this kind of talk before from crazies on the subway, so I wasn't surprised. But then another voice responded . . . in between her rasping breaths. It was deep—like a man who had been smoking his entire life. But it was off somehow, like it had been synthesized to sound human—but wasn't quite right.

"The woman was turned away from me, so I assumed she was making the second voice, too, as people with mental illness often do.

"When her stop came, she practically raced off the train. I caught a glimpse of her face as she passed and there was terror in her eyes. I started to take down some notes about the experience, when something stopped me cold.

"The rasping sound—the breathing I'd heard before—it was still coming from the empty corner of the subway train. There was no one else even close to us. I stared at the corner, feeling my heart thudding in my chest, when suddenly I heard that deep voice again. But this time it was some kind of alien language, a series of grunts and chirps.

"I didn't wait around to find out what it was. I got the hell off that train."

The level of detail in Mason's story stunned Sara. As she looked into his fearful eyes it was clear that he believed every word of it.

"As I researched more about schizophrenia and all of its various types," Mason continued, "I discovered that there has been a steady increase worldwide since the 60s. There is plenty of speculation and controversy over it; some say it's environmental, others say it's genetic, and it's been linked to everything from drug use, to nutritional deficiencies, to vaccines.

"I suppose there may be truth in all of it, but only with classic cases of schizophrenia. What *I'm* saying is that the worldwide increase is due to these goddamn *voices* driving people mad—not chemical imbalances. Hell, for all we know, driving humans mad *is* the whole point."

Sara said, "But not everyone who hears voices goes mad. Some people are able to manage the illness."

"With drugs, yes—if you mean traditional schizophrenia or psychosis. But I'm talking about sane people like you or me, driven to madness by the voices. Nakamura's research showed that some are highly susceptible to the voices—others aren't. But even the most peace-loving person can be driven to violence—all humans are capable of it."

Sara was almost afraid to ask the next question. "What do they . . . you know, the 'voices' . . . say to you?"

Mason looked away, as if suddenly self-conscious. "Deviant things. The kind you think about, but would never actually do. Revenge fantasies, that sort of thing. Much of it better left unsaid."

Sara didn't like where this was going. There was something hidden beneath Mason's vulnerability— something malicious. She thought about their break-up five years ago; it had been ugly to say the least, some might even say hostile.

It was clear now that he *was* schizophrenic, but was he also psychotic? She moved uncomfortably on the loveseat, suddenly aware of Mason's proximity as he faced her. Her body language gave her away.

"Don't worry, Sara. I would never hurt you. They've tried and failed to convince me to hurt others. But now they'll stop at nothing to kill me because I have proof of their existence."

"Proof?"

Mason nodded solemnly. "I've been recording them for a while now. I sewed a mini-video camera into my coat. Sometimes I hide the camera in strategic places and just let it record for hours, particularly in places where the homeless congregate. I've captured the intruder's voices on videotape, several where you can see a person talking to thin air, and a disembodied voice responding. This isn't the first time people have recorded bodiless voices. There are entire books and countless websites dedicated to it. Parapsychologists call it 'electronic voice phenomena.' But they mistakenly think the voices are ghosts or spirits.

"Sometimes they speak in English and other times in some unknown language. I took my recordings to a specialist and was told that it would be physically impossible for human or animal vocal cords to create some of the sounds."

Mason touched Sara's hand, startling her. He said, "Do you want to see it?"

Sara's cheeks blanched. "What do you mean? The videos?"

Mason looked at her as if she'd asked him the most ridiculous question in history. "Of course. I keep the masters with me—there's nowhere safe to hide them. They're always watching me."

Sara's chest tightened uncomfortably. She noticed that her glass was empty and didn't even remember drinking from it. "I really need another one," she said. You want a refill?"

Mason shook his head. "You don't believe a word I'm saying, do you?"

"I believe that you believe it, and that's all that matters right now."

Mason reached into his backpack and pulled out pen and paper. "It's time for me to go. I was able to lose them temporarily, but they'll find me soon enough—they always do."

Sara felt a pang of guilt, letting someone she once cared about leave in such a state . . . and yet, she knew she'd be relieved when he did.

"Listen," Mason said, writing furiously. "I've backed up my videos and uploaded them to a secure storage database. I'm writing down the URL, my username and password. I want you to look it up after I'm gone. Just don't use your home IP address. Use a computer at a public library or one of those Internet cafés."

Sara just stared at him, unsure of what to say.

Mason finished writing down the information, folded the paper and handed it to her. "All I ask is that you watch the videos. If you think there's something to it, and I live long enough, maybe you can help me. I have a few government contacts that might know what to do with the evidence, but I can't get to them while I'm on the run. Just watch the videos, Sara . . . please. Don't let me die for nothing."

A loud *thump* came from above—something on the roof.

What the hell was that?

"Oh Jesus . . . " Mason said, frantically collecting his things. "Physically, they're intangible, but they can make susceptible people do whatever they want. Right now there's a whole group of crazies hunting me."

A large shadow moved across the window next to the front door. Sara held back a scream. She heard hushed whispers, but she couldn't tell where they were coming from. The roof? Outside her front door?

She raced to the kitchen counter and yanked a butcher knife from the rack, then thought better of it and grabbed the meat mallet.

"Call the police!" Mason yelled.

He started toward the door, but never made it. His left cheekbone was crushed instantly by a metal hammer. Screaming, he fell back through the glass coffee table—smashing it in half.

He tried to raise his hands defensively, but it was too late. The hammer came down relentlessly . . . again, again, and again—pulverizing his face, until it looked like it had been run through a meat grinder.

And then, as quickly as it had overtaken her, the rage began to drain from Sara. It was as if a valve had been released inside her and she was suddenly purged from the pain of that traumatic breakup five years ago.

As she stared at the blood pooling around the remains of Mason Tanner's head, it dawned on her that despite years of therapy, she had never really forgiven the bastard.

"It's going to be okay," she said. "Everything is going to be fine now."

And then one heart-stopping moment later, she realized that the voice that had spoken wasn't hers.

The Dark at the End of the Tunnel

"Can he hear me, Doctor?" the incorporeal voice asked.

A second voice answered with a direct tone. "Brain activity is now normal. Give him a few more moments to adjust—after all, there hasn't been any brain activity in ten years."

What the hell are they talking about? he thought.

Suddenly he felt tingling throughout his body. Smells rushed at him. Cheap aftershave. Some sort of industrial antiseptic agent. The unmistakable aroma of cigarette breath. Shapes began to form.

"Welcome back, Mr. Jackson," the first voice said.

～～～

Matt Jackson had no memories of any kind. Everything he'd learned about himself came from Bob Wheeler, his Wealth Management Consultant, and apparently, the only man on Earth who knew anything about him. Matt had no living family, no friends to speak of, and was, to his pleasant surprise, in the top 1% of the wealthiest people in America.

Matt discovered he was one of the ultra-rich; his investment portfolio included gold, high-dividend stocks, real estate and foreign currencies; he would never have to work another day in his life. His home was a secluded mansion in Malibu Canyon surrounded by 30 acres of breathtaking land.

Where had the original wealth come from? Not even Wheeler knew; he wasn't paid to know anything more than what was absolutely essential, namely manage and grow Matt's investments.

Wheeler had been the first voice he'd heard when awoken. He seemed familiar, but there were no specific memories of the man. This was to be expected, he was told by Dr. Smythe, the lead medical advisor at The Cryonic Group. Fragmented memories were a common symptom when awoken from suspended animation. It was a temporary issue, nothing to be concerned about. Smythe expected a full recovery within a matter of weeks.

The memory loss was disturbing, but he took some comfort in knowing it was temporary. Certainly his luxurious lifestyle eased the burden. He was healthy, wealthy—and from this point forward, he could do whatever the hell he wanted.

He wandered around his immense home for several days, trying to get a sense of who he was. There were photos of him throughout the house, traveling the world with various beautiful women on his arm. He searched the Internet for more information on himself, but his personal life was an enigma; he had no blog, website or social media presence to browse. It was downright maddening. He was also stunned at how much had changed in the world during his decade in stasis. The wars in Afghanistan and Iraq, the ascension of China, the recession, the first African American president, high-speed Internet, Wi-Fi, smart phones . . . he could barely keep up with it all.

As he examined the trappings of his life he felt no connection to it. It was unsettling to walk through a stranger's house when the stranger was you. The most disturbing thing was he had no idea why he had voluntarily spent ten years in a stasis chamber. Generally, that was reserved for terminal patients or those already deceased.

Dr. Smythe had informed him that, despite some minimal muscular atrophy that would be addressed with a few months of physical therapy, he was in perfect health. When Matt tried to probe further as to why he had willingly gone into suspended animation, Smythe told him that it was recommended he let his memories return naturally. Forcing them back could cause unnecessary stress and emotional trauma.

He'd reluctantly accepted Smythe's advice, yet the questions nibbled at him like hungry ticks. Where did his money come from? What had happened to his family? Who the fuck was he, really? When the questions became too much to bear, his confusion grew into anger. Finally, he called Bob Wheeler in a fit of rage and threatened to fire him over the phone if he didn't tell him every goddamn thing he knew.

Wheeler finally acquiesced. He told him of a safe hidden inside a baby grand piano that sat covered in the music room of Matt's mansion. He also provided him with the digital password to open the safe. Inside, he told him, was a video recorded 10 years earlier that explained everything.

"Why all the cloak and dagger?" Matt demanded.

"I'm merely following *your* instructions prior to your ten-year sabbatical," Wheeler said. "I was told to inform you about the hidden safe six weeks after you had awoken, or if you demanded it—whichever came first."

Now, as Matt sat in front of his massive entertainment center, with a finger resting on the play button of his remote, apprehension seeped into him like water into sand. Perhaps he was better off not knowing the truth. He had tried to imagine any possible scenario that would explain why he'd gone into suspended animation—but none made sense.

He pressed the play button, and leaned back stiffly on the plush leather couch.

Thirty seconds of static later, a blond, balding man appeared on screen. His eyes were tired looking and familiar. And though his features sagged a bit, it was clear he had been an attractive man in his youth. Matt gasped when the man began to speak—for he realized he was looking at himself. The face was different but the voice and mannerisms were his.

"Hello Matt," he heard the stranger with his voice say. Matt immediately recognized the bookcase in the background; the video had been recorded in the study upstairs.

"If you're watching this video, then most likely, you're looking for answers. What I'm about to tell you . . . well, it may not be easy for you to believe—or even understand. But Dr. Smythe has assured me that full memory recall normally occurs within 4 to 6 weeks of being awakened.

"There's no easy way to say this, so I'm just going to tell you straight. Your given name is Frank Kingston. You're a reclusive multi-millionaire and you're dead. Well, dead to the world, that is. Ten years ago you were in a fatal accident. Fell overboard while drunk on your yacht *The Maximus*. Your body was never recovered."

The VCR remote dropped and clattered onto the beveled glass of the coffee table sitting in front of him. He leaned forward, his mouth slightly agape.

The video continued, "Of course none of that is true—

that's just the fabricated story. Don't worry. I paid top dollar for professionals to handle everything. There's no way to trace anything back to us. I say 'us', because, of course, I am you. I'm the *you* before your facial reconstruction . . . before the hair implants and the liposuction."

The man now named Matt Jackson reached up and touched his hair; gingerly ran his fingers through it. Was this some kind of twisted prank?

"That's right," his former self said. "I'm what you used to look like. But thanks to the modern miracles of plastic surgery, you now look like you. All of the pictures and portraits you see of yourself in the house are doctored photos. They are just part of the tapestry created to bolster our new life.

"It was necessary to start over with a completely new identity. As you can imagine, it would be much too difficult to orchestrate a multi-millionaire disappearing and then reappearing 10 years later. There would be too many questions—too many variables that could get us caught. Having us killed off and starting fresh was the cleanest, most efficient way.

"Which, of course, leads us to the most important question—why?"

Jackson was eager for information yet fearful of what he might learn.

His former self was silent for a moment—as if preparing to deliver bad news. Finally he said, "Why I chose suspended animation is a bit more complicated. And after you watch this tape, make sure you destroy it right aw–"

The image turned to white static.

"What the fu—" Matt yelled.

Frantic, he grabbed the remote and fast-forwarded through the entire tape.

The rest was blank.

It was like the punch line to some perverse practical joke. He noticed his wild-eyed reflection in a large mirror on the wall and began to tug at his unfamiliar features. Everything that had happened since he awoke seemed insane, and yet, as he studied his face in the mirror, he somehow knew it was all true.

Desperation gripped him. He ejected the cassette, wound the loose tape back in with one of the spools, then shoved it back into the VCR and hit the rewind button. In his ten-year absence, VCRs had become outdated technology. This was no more apparent than at this particular moment.

He watched the tape again, this time paying close attention to each and every word. But as before, the tape turned to static at the same place. Had someone erased it on purpose? And if so, why not erase the entire fucking thing?

He fast-forwarded the tape again to make sure he hadn't missed anything. This time the tape froze. He was struck by the time code displayed on the bottom of the screen. It read 00:07:43:07.

What was it about those numbers?

Wait—*Jesus.* It was the pass code numbers to the hidden safe. Now that he thought about it, his street address had the same four numbers: 3747. If you didn't include the zeroes, all three instances had the same numbers.

Fuck this, he thought. *I'm going to get some answers.*

～

The Ferrari F12 Berlinetta was a beautiful machine. And according to the Ferrari website, it was the fastest and most powerful in its history, with a top speed of 210 mph. Matt pushed the Ferrari as fast as he could on the streets of Los Angeles without risking arrest, but it wasn't fast enough.

Finally, he reached Olympic Blvd and looked for the address he'd found online. The Internet had become a frighteningly useful tool in the years since he'd been asleep. A simple web search turned up Bob Wheeler's address in seconds.

It had taken a few minutes to get used to driving again; all of his muscles were still sore from disuse. But it was hardly a chore driving a $300,000 dream machine with all the bells and whistles.

He pulled up in front of Wheeler's home, parked, and glanced at the clock on his dashboard. It was nearly 10:00PM. He didn't care. He'd taken a peek at his accounting books and seen the ungodly fees he was paying the man. As far as he was concerned, for *that* amount of money he could show up whenever he damn well pleased. As he stomped up the front walkway, he thought about all the cryptic doubletalk he'd heard from Dr. Smythe and Bob Wheeler since he'd awoken, and he was sick to death of it. It was time to find out what the hell was going on.

Wheeler wasn't surprised to see him at his doorstep. In fact, he said he'd been expecting him. After all, Matt had no family or friends to speak of. Wheeler was his only real connection to the past. Coming to Wheeler was the obvious choice for a man desperate for answers.

The inside of the townhouse was comfortably spacious. There was nothing extravagant about the furnishings, yet Matt could see that everything was of exceptional quality. This was the home of a man who had nothing to prove. From his furnishings to the books on the shelf, everything seemed functional yet tasteful. Bob Wheeler was a man who spent his money wisely.

Now Wheeler handed him a glass of wine and sat across from him in the study.

Matt nodded his thanks and took a sip. Like everything else in the man's home, the wine was perfect.

"I'm sorry about the video tape," Wheeler said, sitting across from him and crossing his legs leisurely. "Very unfortunate, but out of my hands. You have to understand, I'm on a need to know basis with all of my clients. What they have or haven't done in the past is their concern. My job is to handle your present needs and to ensure your financial future.

"So you know nothing about me?"

"I'm not paid to ask questions. You gave me three specific jobs when you hired me ten years ago: manage your estate, maintain the illusion of your lifestyle for tax and accounting purposes, and arrange for you to be woken up precisely ten years after you went to sleep."

Matt polished off the rest of his wine in two large gulps and sighed heavily. He felt so helpless without his memories. His voice cracked with emotion, "It's just so . . . frustrating not knowing who you are. I feel like I'm hiding from something. It scares me."

Wheeler studied him for a long moment; and then something changed in his eyes. Matt couldn't tell if it was compassion, resignation, or perhaps a little of both. "I can imagine your frustration," Wheeler said. The good news is that, from what Dr. Smythe tells me, your memories will return within weeks.

"What I *can* tell you is that you have no criminal record and no obligations to any family or friends. Your slate is clean and your wealth is spread out globally through low risk, high return investments. It is an enviable position to be in, wouldn't you say?"

"Some would say that, yes," Matt countered.

"You don't approve of your lifestyle?"

"I suppose that depends on your definition."

Wheeler laughed at that. But rather than warming his face, the laughter somehow made him look colder, crueler.

Suddenly Matt felt the need to get out of there—and fast. Wheeler might have been efficient, professional, and a damned genius at financial planning, but one thing he wasn't—was likable.

"Thanks for your time," Matt said without offering his hand. "It's late. I'm sorry I bothered you."

Wheeler rose as leisurely as he'd sat down and gestured toward the front door. "For what you're paying me, Mr. Jackson, it's never a bother."

As Matt took his first steps down the short path toward his Ferrari, Wheeler cleared his throat and said, "There's one more thing."

Matt turned back reluctantly, not wanting to linger a moment longer. "Yes?"

Wheeler's eyes were intense. "You and I only met a few times before you went into stasis. But during our initial meeting at your house, I noticed a leather-bound journal on your desk. You were very protective of it. In fact, you closed the book hurriedly the moment I went near it. If you're looking for answers, I suspect that journal may have some for you. That is, if it still exists."

"That may be helpful. Thank you," Matt said with a terrible attempt at a grin. He turned and walked briskly toward his car.

He felt Wheeler's eyes on his back as he made his way to the driver's side door. Before climbing in, he glanced back at the man standing in the doorway, who was sipping his wine, which under the light of the moon looked thick, dark and viscous.

Two hours and numerous tequila shots later, Matt had managed to wash away much of the uneasiness that had driven him to the dive bar in the first place. The bartender wore an untucked chambray shirt, and had the sleepy, indifferent manner you'd expect from a man who had spent too many nights witnessing the goings on of such a place.

When he had first asked Matt what he wanted to drink, the answer had come naturally and without any thought. He recalled that he enjoyed tequila and Mexican beer. It was the first sign his memory was coming back, and it had provided him with a modicum of relief.

Another welcome distraction was the 40 something year-old woman sitting next to him. Far from a glamour puss, she was attractive enough; probably a knock out in her 20s, he guessed. She had a great rack, blonde hair from a bottle, and as a twice-divorcée living on alimony, admitted that she spent too much of her free time with a drink in her hand. On the plus side, she was sharp, had a sarcastic wit, and was clearly open for seduction. When Matt mentioned that he was independently wealthy, her eyes widened slightly, and curves formed at the corners of her collagen-injected lips.

The bartender began wiping down the bar near them with a knowing look that told Matt he'd seen this scene play out on more than one occasion. "Last call, Mary Beth," he murmured, folding up his grungy bar towel.

"Thanks, Joey," she said and gave the tall man a wry grin.

First name basis, Matt thought. *That can't be good.*

Then again, he was terribly lonely and horny—mostly horny—and didn't much care about the woman's past. He wasn't in the market for a wife; he just wanted to avoid another night alone.

The Dark at the End of the Tunnel

Mary Beth leaned in seductively and whispered in his ear. "You okay to drive?"

〜

Matt had no respect for Mary Beth, but he had to admit she was a lot of fun. She even managed to make him laugh a few times with her off-color jokes. But that laughter ended suddenly when a naked, blood-covered black man leapt out into the street—right in front of them. Matt slammed on his brakes, causing the Ferrari to shudder violently until it stopped—missing the large man by inches.

Mary Beth slammed back into her seat. "What the hell?" she yelled.

Matt gazed into the man's terror-filled eyes. They seemed to be pleading for help.

A gunshot rang out. The left side of the man's head exploded, spraying the windshield with a fine red mist.

"Jesus Christ!" Matt punched the accelerator, hurling Mary Beth back into her seat again, tires screeching in protest.

"What is wrong with you?" she demanded.

"Me?" He shouted back, louder than he meant. He downshifted and turned onto the first residential street he saw, trying to get as much distance as possible from what he'd seen. "We could've been killed back there!"

"What? I didn't see anything!"

"You didn't—" It was clear from the look on Mary Beth's face that she was telling the truth. This was, of course, impossible, since at the very least she should have seen the blood splatter across the windshield.

What blood? another part of his mind asked, as his eyes searched the glass for even a speck of it.

The windshield was spotless. It didn't make any sense. What the hell just happened?

"What did you see?" Mary Beth asked. "What was it?"

But Matt couldn't think of how to respond without sounding like a lunatic. If what he'd seen was real, there was no way she could've missed it. And since there was no blood residue on the windshield, he questioned whether he'd seen anything himself.

Hallucination? Dr. Smythe had warned him hallucinations were a *possible* side effect, but a remote possibility at best.

So he said, "I'm not feeling too good. I should take you home."

And he did.

Mary Beth lived adjacent to Beverly Hills in a small, but well-kept two-story condo. Matt's intention had been to drop her off and go home, but she'd insisted he come in for a drink. He wasn't sure if she was an unusually forgiving person or just desperate to get laid—but he decided not to examine it too closely.

A night with an attractive stranger sure as hell beat going home to an empty bed. And if he were lucky, it just might take his mind off that man's exploding head. He and Mary Beth enjoyed a couple more drinks together, which helped take the edge off.

Matt was lost in thought when a seductive whisper from behind him said, "Care to join me?"

He turned just in time to catch a glimpse of blonde hair and Mary Beth's black negligee as she wafted into the master bedroom.

He downed the rest of his drink like a shot and set the glass down—right next to a stack of letters on a vintage patina table. His eyes widened as he caught a glimpse of the numbers in Mary Beth's address: 3747.

Those same four numbers again. A different order—but they were the same four numbers all right.

Matt wasn't superstitious—at least he didn't think he was—but something wasn't right. Every shred of intuition told him to get out of there. He took a deep breath, ran his fingers through his hair, and prepared to ask for a rain check.

The master bedroom was dark and quiet; the moon cast eerie shadows through the window over a large four-poster bed that took up most of the space.

"Listen . . . " he said, and his voice cracked when he said it. "I'm not feeling well and—"

The blood everywhere stopped him cold; it looked as if someone had sprayed the walls with it using a hose.

But that wasn't the worst part.

Mary Beth's body was splayed across the bed; it had been split open from her neck down. Her glistening intestines were stretched out from her abdomen and had been used to tie her arms and legs to the bedposts.

And then somehow, impossibly . . . the dead woman turned her broken neck into an impossible angle, until her bloated face was grinning at him with a knowing look.

It wasn't Mary Beth.

Matt fell back and screamed; he smashed into a bookcase and caused it to collapse with a crash.

The door to the master bedroom's bathroom flung open and Mary Beth came scrambling out, wild-eyed. She was still wearing the black negligee and holding a silver-handled brush matted with blonde hair.

Matt glanced over at the bed and saw it was empty, and perfectly made.

"Are you fucking crazy?" Mary Beth yelled.

He didn't answer her; he was too busy running from her home.

Matt spent the next two days at home in a drunken haze, taking advantage of the full bar at his disposal. But no amount of alcohol could wash away the hallucinations, which had become increasingly gruesome; every conceivable kind of torture and mutilation, visited upon an array of ghostly victims, and without any context. He had placed several frantic calls to Dr. Smythe, but according to his unhelpful answering service, the good doctor was out of the country for several weeks on business.

In between drunken rages and bouts of uncontrollable sobbing, Matt searched every nook and cranny of his sizable mansion for the journal Wheeler had described. Not finding it only spurred more outrage and drunkenness.

On the third day, he woke up on top of the billiards table in the game room with a loaded gun in his hand. He'd found it the night before, hidden behind some bottles on the top shelf of his bar. He carried it around the house for several hours and had seriously considered using it on himself—then passed out.

Now, as he glanced around the game room, there was a growing sense of familiarity. And despite a horrendous hangover, that familiarity made him feel a little better. He glanced at a *Star Wars* pinball machine in the corner, and suddenly remembered the day he'd gotten the high score. A rack of CDs against the wall, including the entire *Led Zeppelin* collection, brought back pleasant memories, too. He could feel his identity returning, moment by precious moment. Carnal images flashed through his mind. There had been women, oh yes. He could see their faces in a twisted kaleidoscope of memories, each perversion more disturbing than the last.

THE DARK AT THE END OF THE TUNNEL

What kind of person had he been? Curiosity ate at him, yet he was afraid to look too closely. Another flash of memory and he remembered hiding other weapons besides the gun. Yes . . . he *was* starting to remember! He could see an image . . . a dungeon of some kind.

He leapt to his feet and began to run—it was all coming back now. There was a hidden room built beneath the house, only accessible by a trap door. As soon as he reached the study in the northernmost room of the first floor, he knew exactly where to look. He knelt down, grabbed the edge of a massive Oriental rug and flipped it over.

He recognized a particular floorboard and yanked it loose. Underneath was a small, but sturdy wooden handle. Eagerly, he heaved the trap door open, revealing a set of dust-covered steps leading down into a pool of darkness.

Nothing good would come from going down there. Somehow he knew this. And yet, he also knew it was inevitable that he descend.

As he stepped down into the blackness, he remembered a light switch at the bottom of the stairs. He braced himself as he turned on the lights. It didn't make a bit of difference; what he saw there shook him to his core. In that one moment of recognition, he knew that despite his new name, new face, and fabricated life, nothing could change what he was and always would be.

∿

In a locked cabinet against the back wall of the secret room, Matt found the journal Wheeler had described. It didn't take long to figure out the lock combination: 3-7-47.

Inside the cabinet were stacks upon stacks of journals—some going back hundreds of years. Some were written on tattered notepads while others sported fine leather covers. The oldest was written on parchment.

He spent all day and that night poring through them and the intimate details of nine different people's lives, starting in the mid-1600s and ending ten years prior, the day he went into suspended animation.

He was all of them. Only the names and circumstances had changed.

James Dowle, his original name, a Puritan from East Anglia in England, had moved his family—his wife and two children—to Salem, Massachusetts in 1676. His unfortunate streak of luck began with the loss of his wife Abigail to smallpox in early '77, followed by his 6 year-old son Isaac and 4 year-old daughter Mary. He soon contracted the sickness, too, and in desperation, sought out a healer reputed to cure the incurable—for a price.

A secret meeting was planned, as this was not long before the Salem witch trials, and any unorthodox practices at that time were suspect. He paid the old woman his entire life savings for a powerful spell of healing.

To his amazement, it worked.

Having survived the smallpox scare, Dowle came up with a plan to reclaim the money he'd paid the old hag. He showed up at her home one evening a week later, demanding that she return his money—otherwise he threatened to accuse her of practicing witchcraft, a crime punishable by death. When she refused, he slit her throat and ransacked her home, stealing a small fortune, and an ancient book containing everything from love spells to good fortune hexes, to demonic curses.

It was at this point, while reading the first and oldest journal, that Matt finally remembered the significance of the numbers that had been haunting him. April 3rd, 1677

(4/3/77) was the date Dowle had used the book of spells to summon a powerful and nameless demon. It appeared to him as a formless entity, like living black smoke. The only discernible features were its nine glowing eyes, which glowed like burning embers. It promised him nine lives of wealth, power, and influence, as well as the retention of his memories from each previous life. Upon his ninth death, the demon would return to claim his soul.

To maintain the spell's effects, Dowle was required to sacrifice a human being once a year on the anniversary of the pact. This pleased him greatly as it gave him the excuse he needed to unleash the bloodlust he'd suppressed his entire life. He far exceeded the amount of killing necessary to maintain his pact; his list of victims throughout his nine lives numbered in the thousands.

With great wealth came the ability to build secret torture chambers, constructed within the depths of his castles, châteaux, and colonial mansions over the next few centuries. His positions of power and influence generally kept him above suspicion. And on the rare occasion that he had come under scrutiny, he'd used his vast resources to pay off, discredit, or kill anyone whom he considered a threat.

Throughout all nine lives, he had searched for a loophole in the demon's pact, and finally, in his life as multi-millionaire Frank Kingston, he had. A combination of technology and mystical knowledge was his salvation; a way to protect his soul—by releasing it into the limbo between life and death. The answer was suspended animation. It would cause all bodily functions to cease, and untether his soul from its human vessel. It would be out of reach of the demon, forcing it to return to its dimension empty-handed, unless it was ever summoned again.

The plan had worked. Goddamn if it hadn't! Now he

was unfrozen and alive again, free of the demon and eager to enter a new pact—with a different entity. He glanced around at the dungeon he'd built and examined some of the torturous devices lined up against the bloodstained walls: thumbscrews, a Pear of Anguish, a Breast Ripper—even a custom-made Iron Maiden. Memories of the men, women and children he'd tortured mercilessly and slain floated through his mind. Recollections came slowly at first—like specters. He remembered the nigger who had managed to escape the dungeon in his colonial mansion that night in 1803. He'd quickly caught up to the man and blown his brains out on the private road leading to his plantation. This was the spectral reenactment he'd witnessed on the highway a few days ago. Not a hallucination. Not a ghost.

He recalled the woman he'd seen sliced open in Mary Beth's bedroom. In a previous life as a brothel owner in Paris, he had choked the woman to death with her own intestines. She had dared to scratch his face when he'd tried to rape her and he'd made her pay for it dearly. He had loved that woman; or something as close to love as he could fathom.

He pushed those thoughts out of his mind. He was now more vulnerable than he'd been in centuries. Without the protection of a pact, if he somehow died, he wouldn't be resurrected a tenth time. He needed to summon another demon quickly, and that would require a fresh kill. Perhaps that whore Mary Beth he'd met in the bar. She lived alone; she was an easy target. Then again, that bartender who had seen them together might remember his face if the police investigated—so perhaps that wasn't the best idea.

A phone rang from upstairs, startling him. It was the first time he'd heard it. Who could be calling at this time of night?

He raced up the stairs to catch the caller before they hung up, excited at the prospect of someone from his past calling.

"Hello?" he said breathlessly into the receiver.

Silence.

Straining, he could hear breathing on the other end of the line.

"Who is this?" Matt demanded.

"Dr. Smythe," a familiar voice answered.

Matt ground his teeth. "About goddamn time you returned my call."

"Listen," the doctor said. "I need to see you right away. I have to talk to you in person. The phone isn't safe."

Matt said, "Isn't safe? What are you–"

"Tonight at the clinic. I'm the only one on duty."

Matt grew more suspicious. "I want answers, Smythe."

"Don't worry. You'll get them . . . I know things."

The next thing Matt heard was a dial tone.

Matt struggled to remember any details about Dr. Smythe—certain parts of his memory still remained fuzzy. He vaguely remembered procuring the doctor's services, and paying him a king's ransom for his discretion.

He wondered how he'd found Smythe in the first place—possibly through Wheeler.

I know things. Those were his last words on the phone. Matt didn't like the implication; if Smythe knew anything incriminating he would have to be disposed of.

Matt grabbed his gun before he left, realizing this new situation might work to his advantage. After all, he was in need of a fresh victim in order to summon a demon again.

Matt arrived at the clinic an hour later to find the front door unlocked and wide open.

He'd already been tense, but now he was getting downright jumpy. He didn't like being exposed in this way; he liked more control over his victims. He reached into the large front pocket of his winter coat and wrapped his hands around the Glock .9mm hidden there.

"Hello," he called out as he entered the tenebrous, empty lobby. His voice echoed back, cold and hollow. Matt felt the walls by the door for a light switch but found none.

In his left hand he carried a knapsack filled with the specific materials he would need to conjure another demon. The dungeon in his mansion had been filled with every conceivable herb, root, gemstone, aromatic, and occult ingredient imaginable. The sooner he could enter into a new pact the better. He wasn't comfortable in his current unprotected state; for the first time in centuries, death would be permanent.

He locked the clinic door from the inside and pulled out his gun. There was an oddly familiar scent in the air, but he couldn't quite place it. "Dr. Smythe!" he called out and ventured deeper into the shadows.

Despite the uncomfortably cold temperature, sweat slid down his temples. He started to think he'd made a mistake coming here in the first place, but realized he'd probably never get a better chance at the doctor alone.

He moved farther into the darkened hallway; it was dimly lit at the other end by what he guessed was a red light just beyond his view. It cast a faint, eerie glow across the walls. His throat felt more constricted with each step he took.

A moment later he nearly cried out in fear when he noticed a dark figure standing motionless at the end of hall.

It was a nude female with long, disheveled hair backlit in crimson.

"Hel . . . hello," he croaked, his throat feeling bone dry.
The figure remained deathly still.

"Look, I don't know who you are, but I've got a gun." *Where the hell was Smythe?*

A hideous, unidentifiable sound erupted from the woman's throat and she began to move toward him. When the light caught her just right, he could see that her face had been savagely carved off.

He had done that to many pretty girls.

Yet this hallucination didn't vanish quickly like the previous ones had. As she drew closer with outstretched arms, he could smell her rotting corpse. He fired his gun and a bullet blew a hole through her neck, exposing the cartilage and muscle underneath. The faceless woman staggered from the impact, and then reached for him again—her fingers curled like claws.

Matt took a step back, about to fire at her again when he felt a terrible pain in his right calf. A boy drenched in blood—no more than 5 years old—was biting into his leg like a wild animal.

He shot several bullets into the child's head until it resembled the remains of a smashed bowl that had been filled with jelly. He took note that the lower half of young the boy was missing. The little bastard was one of countless children he'd torn in two on the rack over the centuries. It was one of his great delights. But the sight of it now—rotted flesh and all—was turning his stomach.

At the end of the hall, more silhouettes appeared. Four . . . then eight . . . then so many he lost count. A handful of them were headless.

He emptied his rounds into the growing horde, watched some of them jerk back as the bullets slammed into them. The sound of gunfire in the confined space stung his ears.

Silently, they kept coming.

He felt his knapsack slip from his fingers . . . heard the contents spill onto the ground. But he ignored it, his thoughts only on survival now.

He ran the other way, wincing at the bleeding wound in his calf. How could a hallucination bite him like that? *It wasn't possible!*

As he raced for the lobby, he noticed more lumbering figures blocking his path—trying to cut him off.

He veered toward the right and into another dark hallway, panic rising in him. *Godammit, there has to be an emergency exit!*

Just ahead was a glass door; *Authorized Personnel Only* was emblazoned on it.

He hit the door running and it swung open wide. He recognized where he was immediately: the main chamber for body storage. He spun and closed the door, locking it from the inside. The chilly temperature in the room was almost painful; he huddled into his jacket for warmth. The rows of cryo-units reminded him of shiny, metal coffins. A wave of claustrophobia swept over him; he had spent a decade inside one of those loathsome things.

The mob of animated corpses reached the thick glass door and began to claw at it, smearing it with blood and other bodily fluids. The face of a young girl in front was smashed against the glass; there were two jagged holes where her eyes used to be.

The door wouldn't hold them for long.

A strange, unearthly sound emanated from behind him. He spun around to see thick black smoke swirling around him as if alive. He recognized it immediately and started to scream—but it caught in his throat, his vocal chords paralyzed. In fact, he couldn't move any muscles at all.

Smoke continued to gather like the clouds of a terrible storm and formed into a human shape—that of Dr. Smythe. His hardened face twitched and his lips gave way to the faintest hint of satisfaction.

"Don't you think it's time to end this charade?" Smythe said, and the voice was as cold as his narrowed eyes. He appeared to float toward Matt, stopping barely an inch from his face. The stench caused him to choke; a smell he now recognized as sulfur. It was exuding from the demon's mouth.

"Your doublecross was well-thought out," it said. "I'll give you that. But you didn't read our contract, did you? It binds us in every way—we are symbiotic. I was aware of your deceitful plans the moment you thought of them.

"In fact, I'm not here. I'm in your mind. Everything you've experienced is by design, an intricate drama starring you as the lead, while everyone you've encountered were extras and supporting players. I gave you the worst thing imaginable . . . the hope of happiness and freedom . . . just so I could strip it all away and reveal the truth of what you really are."

Tears began to spill from Matt's eyes. For he knew that everything the nameless demon said was true.

"I can read your thoughts now. You're terrified of going back into that cryo-unit for all of eternity." A grin spread across the demon's face. "But that's the best part."

Matt struggled to understand.

"Don't you see?" the demon laughed. "You never left it to begin with."

It was then that Matt noticed the silver nameplate above the nearest cryo-unit. It read:

CRYO-UNIT 7734
MATTHEW JACKSON
STATUS: IN STASIS

Matt was no longer a tangible form. He felt his consciousness still *inside* the cryo-unit. He struggled against it, desperate to maintain the illusion, to keep his physical form outside the metal coffin.

The cold fear of what was coming rose in him; trapped forever inside his body, unable to move, yet conscious of every moment. There would be no end. No death. No light at the end of any tunnel.

There would only be the dark.

The hallucinations had never existed. *He* was the hallucination.

As the last of his consciousness returned to the blackness within the stasis chamber, his vision inverted. From this new perspective, he saw the engraved numbers on his nameplate, and finally understood their true meaning.

7734 upside down spelled hƐᒪᒪ.

ACKNOWLEDGEMENTS

As I prepared to write this, I was surprised to learn that a great number of people have strong feelings about acknowledgement pages. This epiphany came after digging through various online articles, blog posts and forum discussions about what makes a good acknowledgments page.

Some were emphatic that no one reads them, yet others expressed their love of reading them. There were some strong opinions about what should and shouldn't be included in an acknowledgments page, and they were often contradictory. So ultimately, I decided that the only thing that mattered was that I remained authentic in my writing of it.

Here goes . . .

Firstly, there's my mother, Beverly. Her passion for films and books greatly inspired my own love of stories. And while she has long since passed on to whatever awaits us on the other side, my appreciation for her has only grown—not waned. In my youth, she often read my clunky attempts at fiction, seemingly without judgment and always with gentle encouragement. I got better, mom—I promise.

I am deeply thankful to friends and family who read early drafts of most of these stories, long before I considered submitting them for publication. They include my wife Samantha, Josh Galitsky, Robbie Hyman, Michelle Clot Cook, Christopher Ransom, Stephen Gordon and

Joanna Moctezuma. Though we have lost touch, sweet Joanna, your genuine enthusiasm for my fiction during some of my darkest hours will never be forgotten.

A special acknowledgment goes out to editor/author John Kenny, who accepted my first story (which literally brought tears to my eyes); he also became my freelance editor of choice. It was John's editorial tutelage that gave me the confidence to keep submitting my work to publishers.

The list of people that have encouraged me, either in person or online, could fill several pages, and I am grateful to each and every one of them. However, there are those who, for reasons known only to them, have been the biggest supporters of my work. They include Christi Wynn, Stacey McKeever, Michele Clot Cook, Mike Tunison, Dana Moreshead, Allen Simpson, Chad Foushee, R.J. Cavender, Elita Toscano, Ian Scheller, fellow authors Christopher Ransom, Robert S. Wilson, John Palisano, and close friend Roy Johansen. Your words of encouragement and support of my work meant everything.

I have a great deal of respect and gratitude for Joe Mynhardt, the visionary behind Crystal Lake Publishing. Joe is a class act, an incredibly hard worker, and a multi-talented editor, author and publisher. It is an honor to have my collection published by him. Special thanks to everyone at Crystal Lake, especially Emma Audsley and Paula Limbaugh, and the wonderful proofreaders, Linzi Osburn, Lex Jones, and Devin Anderson.

I must also thank my friends and supporters over at Cemetery Dance Publishing for releasing the eBook version of this collection. I have the deepest respect and admiration for my editor over there, Norman Prentiss, as well as Brian James Freeman, and of course, Founder and Publisher

Richard Chizmar, whose faith in my work remains one of the milestones of my career.

There wouldn't be an acknowledgments page or even a book, if not for Samantha Grant, my incredible wife, whose belief and encouragement over the years has never wavered. And of course, a warm thank you to my son Zane, whose unconditional love and faith in me has a special magic of its own.

Perhaps most importantly, I must thank you, the reader of this book. For amidst the seemingly endless sea of entertainment options, you have chosen to read my collection. And for that, you have my eternal gratitude.

ABOUT THE AUTHOR

Taylor Grant is a Bram Stoker Award Nominated author, award-winning filmmaker, professional screenwriter, award-winning copywriter, and part-time actor. He lives in Los Angeles with his wife and son.

Find out more at www.taylorgrant.com

The End?

Not at all.

If you enjoyed this book, be sure to check out other Crystal Lake Publishing books for your Dark Fiction, Horror, Suspense, and Thriller needs.

We hope you enjoyed this title. If so, we'd be grateful if you could leave a review on your blog or any of the other websites and outlets open to book reviews. Reviews are like gold to writers and publishers, since word-of-mouth is and will always be the best way to market a great book. And remember to keep an eye out for more of our books.

CONNECT WITH CRYSTAL LAKE PUBLISHING

Website:
www.crystallakepub.com
(receive a free eBook if you join our mailing list)
Facebook:
www.facebook.com/Crystallakepublishing
Twitter:
https://twitter.com/crystallakepub

With unmatched success over the last two years, Crystal Lake Publishing is quickly becoming the go-to press for Dark Fiction authors and fans. We publish the highest quality Dark Fiction books and poetry collections, which include Horror, Sci-Fi, Fantasy, Thrillers, Suspense, Supernatural, and Noir.

Crystal Lake Publishing puts integrity, honor and respect at the forefront of our operations.

We strive for each book and outreach program that's launched to not only entertain and touch or comment on issues that affect our readers, but also to strengthen and support the Dark Fiction field and its authors.

Not only do we publish authors who are legends in the field and as hardworking as us, but we look for men and women who care about their readers and fellow human beings. We only publish the very best Dark Fiction, and look forward to launching many new careers.

We strive to know each and every one of our readers, while building personal relationships with our authors, reviewers, bloggers, pod-casters, bookstores and libraries.

Crystal Lake Publishing is and will always be a beacon

of what passion and dedication, combined with overwhelming teamwork and respect, can accomplish: Unique fiction you can't find anywhere else.

We do not just publish books, we present you worlds within your world, doors within your mind, from talented authors who sacrifice so much for a moment of your time.

This is what we believe in. What we stand for. This will be our legacy.

Welcome to Crystal Lake Publishing.

We hope you enjoyed this title. If so, we'd be grateful if you could leave a review on your blog or any of the other websites and outlets open to book reviews. Reviews are like gold to writers and publishers, since word-of-mouth is and will always be the best way to market a great book. And remember to keep an eye out for more of our books.

THANK YOU FOR PURCHASING THIS BOOK